MW00990389

Swallowed Ashes
Victoria's Journey

Meredith Baldwin

Saguaro Books, LLC
SB
Arizona

Saguaro Books, LLC
16845 E. Avenue of the Fountains, Ste. 325
Fountain Hills, AZ 85268
www.saguarobooks.com

ISBN: 9798691710056
Library of Congress Cataloging Number
LCCN: 2020947323
Printed in the United States of America
First Edition

Dedication

I dedicate this book to several people. My younger self for having this cool idea of a girl who goes swimming and ends up swallowing the ashes of a dead person, becoming possessed and actually writing it down for me to find many years later. For my husband, Mike, who always believes in my escapist fantasies without judgment. For my cheerleaders Marisa, Scarlet, Isla, Juliette, Locklen and even Malibu who keep me going. And finally, for my parents who are always there to listen to just one more sentence. HA!

Thank you to Saguaro Books, LLC for this incredible opportunity to have others read my story.

Prelude

She has rejected the light. It was the most beautiful thing she had ever seen but at what cost? To merely hover over her own ashes?

She hoped the wind would pick up soon and carry her down the lake. She can't stay bound to her ashes forever. She has to find a host—someone to help her with her unfinished business. She had to find the person who killed her.

Chapter 1

Finally, My Day Off

I woke up twenty minutes ago but can't seem to move my legs to get off this bed. Instead, I am laying here staring at the cherry blossom mural my mom painted years ago. I always think of cherry blossoms in a romantic way. Maybe most people prefer roses but a cherry blossom is a much better way to say, "I love you." I imagine strolling down a sidewalk, hand in hand, with the love of my life. Nowhere is more romantic than the park in the spring, with the cherry trees surrounding us. That would be the perfect time for him to get down on one knee. I close my eyes to get a clearer picture of the man, the man I have been in love with for three years. He has no idea this will be the way he proposes to me but it's fun to think about the moment in advance. All of a sudden, someone barreling up the stairs brings me into reality. I can only guess who it is.

My door flies open. Piper, my best friend, comes barging in and lands on my bed. Although I am completely surprised by her visit, I still can't seem to move.

"What the heck are you doing in bed? It's 10 o'clock. I got out of work a few minutes early this morning. How come you didn't call me yesterday? I left you like seven messages." Piper stands over me with her hands on her hips while I'm lying flat on my stomach, my face smushed into my pillow with my cheek chubbed up. I only move my eyes to look at her and respond with a moan.

"Are you sick?" she asks, with a concerned look. She grabs my right shoulder to jostle me. If I were sick, that sort of contact would not be appreciated.

"Nooo, I'm not sick," I mumble.

"Scoot over," Piper exclaims. She grabs my arm and torso, turning me on my back. She lies down beside me. When my older sister, Valentina, went to a four-year college last year, I absolutely traded up and took her full-sized bed. I still get dirty looks from her when she comes home to visit, even though, I always graciously give her my room with her old bed back and take back my reject of a twin bed in her old room. Luckily for me, she had a job this summer and I only had to vacate my room for a long weekend back in July.

"Why didn't you call me back yesterday?" Piper asks again.

"Because I've been working nonstop with the shifts I had to cover, including yours, so I got home late." I try to stifle a yawn but it comes out anyway. I close my eyes and ask her what I know she's dying to tell me. "How was your date?" I ask, sincerely.

"Oh, my gosh, it was awesome. He took me to Cavanaugh's Grill."

He, being her newest boyfriend, Grant.

"Oooh," I open my eyes, while salivating and give her a jealous scowl.

She continues with a smirk, "I wanted the fish tacos so badly but I didn't want to smell fishy all night so I got the gourmet grilled cheese. It was delish." She lets out a smittened sigh and smiles big. Her chestnut brown hair is extra cute today. Probably still styled from yesterday's date. All throughout high school, it was long and straight; flat-ironed, constantly. This spring she decided to chop it off and now it's about shoulder length. She must have curled it yesterday, because it is bouncy and wavy.

"I'm happy you had a good time." My stomach can no longer remain silent. It growls. "Now I'm hungry," I say, exasperated. I was hoping to sleep at least half of the day.

"Good, now maybe you'll get out of bed and I can tell you about my hot date."

"There's more than gooey grilled cheese?" I tease, while she hops off the bed and gives me a hand. I slowly rise, feeling all the kinks in my back and feet from working so much.

"Oh, there's a lot more than gooey grilled cheese," she states, insinuating a very juicy story coming up.

"Don't say anything inappropriate if my mom is downstairs," I give her a warning glance.

Piper gasps, "Victoria Rose, I wouldn't dare." She gives me a fake evil glare and her tone is challenging. I immediately start to worry. She is always trying to rile my parents and make them uncomfortable. I sigh, knowing I'm in for an eventful breakfast as we head downstairs.

My mom is squatting under the sink grabbing some cleaning supplies and my dad is at work. My parents are both teachers and, of course, have the summer off; but my dad always works at Rick's Hardware to make extra money. He's a natural born carpenter but he combined his love of teaching and carpentry to teach shop class. This town is small, so my dad got lucky and teaches English for a few periods of the day and is the shop teacher the other half. Shop class is an elective; most kids choose theater or home economics. I, of course, took shop class. I can make an awesome birdhouse. Because he was the only shop teacher, the school allowed me to be in his class. For English, though, they made me have another teacher. I was so jealous of my friends. My dad always interacted with the class and made it fun. He did impressions and told funny stories. It was such a bummer to not get to experience that.

It seems my mom has been busy all morning. There are fresh flowers on the entryway table, the hardwood floors are gleaming and it smells of lemons and Clorox. Our house is small but it's well-kept and cozy. I love it. I am not looking forward to leaving for college in a few weeks, because it means living on campus and not here.

"Hey, mom," I say quietly, so I don't scare her.

"Morning, Victoria. Did I wake you with the vacuum?" she asks.

"Oh, no. It wasn't you." I glare straight into Piper's eyes but she could care less.

"Morning, Piper." Mom says, lovingly with a smile.

"Good morning, Lily. I went straight up to V's room when you were vacuuming, I didn't want to bother you."

"What are you girls up to today?" Mom asks, while spraying the counter with cleaner.

"Nothing," I state,

At the same time Piper enthusiastically says, "School shopping."

"Huh? What?" I slump my shoulders, knowing I have no say in today's plans. I mosey over to the cabinet to fetch a bowl.

"We have to get stuff for college. One of my professor's wants me to get a graphing calculator, I need a thumb drive, paper and we need to get fake I.D.s."

I scowl at her. Mom stops wiping the counter and looks up.

"Just kidding; but, seriously, all those other supplies are necessary. I can't believe we waited until the last minute. We leave in two weeks, V. Two weeks."

"I know, Pipe. I just keep working and working. You know, filling in for people who keep asking off. I never have time to go and get school supplies."

"Well, today you have time. It's your day off."

After offering to get Piper breakfast, who refuses, I get my cereal and sit down.

"Tell me about your date," I insist. Mom grabs her bucket of cleaning supplies and heads to the guest bathroom. No doubt she's giving us privacy, as she doesn't want to hear anything about Pipe's date.

"So, Grant picked me up around 4 o'clock and we went to play mini-golf. We got snow cones. They didn't have those spoon-straw things and let me tell you," she looks pretty darn serious and holds both her hands up as if halting traffic, "there is no dainty way to eat a snow cone. It kept touching my nose. It was irritating." She crinkles her nose, probably recalling the cold annoyance.

I laugh at the thought. "I'm sure he didn't notice. I have the most brilliant question though." I put a huge spoonful of cereal in my mouth.

"What's that?" she waits as I chew.

"What flavor did he get?"

She gives me a puzzled look. I love how she can raise only one eyebrow. I've never been able to do that.

"Why is that a brilliant question?"

"It will tell us a lot about his personality."

"Which flavors mean what?" she indulges me.

"If he got lime, maybe he's pretty chill."

"No, not lime." she smiles, understanding my game.

"Grape, maybe, arrogant," she shakes her head, "piña colada, he bats for the other team," serious faced, she interjects immediately, "Absolutely not. Trust me," she gives me a sly crooked smile.

"All right, all right. Moving on," I wave my hands at her, shooing her insinuations.

"Bubblegum, he's immature," she shakes her head again, "cherry, he wants to have many babies."

"Aahh," she throws her head back, laughing.

"Oh, no. Many babies?" I ask, giggling back.

"Yeah. Oh, great."

"What flavor did you get?"

14

"Arrogant and babies." We both laugh so hard we're crying. We may be strange but we get each other. We've always clicked. She continues to tell me about her date, while I finish eating.

"So who won?" I ask, taking my bowl to the dishwasher.

"Won what?" Piper looks at me, confused.

"Putt-Putt, nerd," I tease.

"He did. It ticked me off, too. I couldn't get the stupid ball through the dinosaur's legs. It kept hitting his toe."

I snicker at the level of her anger, although I know she does this for my comedic benefit.

"That sucks. I know how you like to win," I give her an apologetic smile, knowing in her fake fit of rage, she does like to win.

"No worries, I whacked it in the shin."

"Grant?"

"No, that stupid dinosaur."

"Oh, geez."

"Uh, he deserved it," she states as matter of fact and raises her eyebrows at me, completing that topic of conversation.

"So, you think he'll ask you out again or are you gonna ask him out?" We head back up the stairs, so I can get dressed.

"I think it went rather well. It is Thursday already, huh?"

"Yep." I slip on my white shorts and navy tee and go in search of my brown loafers.

"I guess if I wanna see him, I better make plans."

"Absolutely. Maybe jet skiing tomorrow after work?"

15

"That's perfect, V." Piper's parents have loads of money. Therefore, they have all the fun things in life like Jet Skis, snow skis, boats, all the hunting gear imaginable, motorcycles and go-karts. Yes, go-karts are in their shed.

"Wait, I should ask him if he wants to meet me at the bonfire Saturday night."

"Duh. I keep forgetting about that. OK, I'm ready. Where the heck are my sunglasses?"

We head out to Piper's car, hop in and set off to the local we-carry-everything-store.

Piper's parents didn't want her to be too cocky at school by giving her a brand new beamer, so they bought her a two year-old one. Yeah, no such luck. She's still cocky and had by far the best car at school.

Piper never disappoints, she has one of my favorite rock bands playing in her car. We have always had the same taste in music and I think that's one of the main things that kept us connected through the awkward middle school years. We've known each other since preschool but have been best friends for about eight years. Because of our long-standing friendship, her parents are also great friends with my parents. Our families have even gone on summer vacations together. It's been pretty awesome that it all works out.

Piper starts air drumming while still driving straight, holding the wheel with her knee and I play the air guitar. We make a great air band.

"Chop Suey. What a funny name," I say, as we get out of the car.

Swallowed Ashes

Out of breath from our concert performance, we go into the store, where they play no music at all. Boooo.

We only have to go to one store to get our school supplies. Luckily, Piper's cousin works there and he directs us to every item on our list. We go window-shopping for fun. As we walk to the car, Piper has an idea.

"I should ask Grant if he wants to go shoot darts then go to the bonfire Saturday night."

"That sounds awesome."

Piper is into every sport. Grant is one lucky guy, if he likes a shooting range over a movie and a long walk on the beach. I think if Piper had to do anything involving a beach, it would consist of surfing or beach volleyball.

"Do you think Ryan will be there?" Piper asks.

I freeze at the car door and look up at her. She gives me a sly look, leading me to believe she knows something I don't.

"Ryan MacKenna? Why would you think he would be there?" I try to hide my surging excitement not taking the hook she was baiting. Pipe knows me better than my ill attempt at acting casually in the presence of Ryan MacKenna's name.

"Maybe Grant mentioned it?" she lies, coolly.

"What the heck do you know that I don't? Is he back from vacation?" I'm still trying to measure my excitement but I am losing control.

"Maybe," she ducks her head in the car, getting in.

"Piper, is he back?" I almost whack my head, jumping in.

"He gets back tomorrow. You know, you might actually try talking to him."

"He knows who I am, too, ya know," I state sourly. I guess the part I forgot to mention is the man I've loved for three years, is Ryan MacKenna. We have had a few classes together over the years and, sometimes, have seen each other at school events but there was never a time I told him how I felt. He dated girls and I dated some boys yet the timing was never right. By golly, this is the time. *I have no fear in asking him out and no fear of rejection. I'm smart, I'm eighteen, I'm tan and I'm single. There's no way he'll say no. Right?*

"Well, he's probably going to the bonfire but I can tell Grant to make sure he is there and I'll leave it all to you, girlfriend." Piper, being as feisty as she is, has threatened multiple times to tell him I like him, so she doesn't have to hear me whine about him anymore. Every time, I plead with her not to say anything because I want it to happen naturally. She reluctantly caves, every time.

I smile and start daydreaming about our romantic evening at the bonfire. Holding hands, sharing cotton candy and maybe even a good night kiss…

"What should I wear?" I cut off my daydreaming.

"White looks great on you, especially since you're tanned."

"What about the pink dress I wore to my parents' anniversary dinner?"

"I like that one; but it's a smidge fancy for a bonfire."

"Right."

"Your yellow one would look great. You'll just have to try some of them on and we'll see.

Want to change and go to the lake? We need a nice glow before Saturday." Piper starts the car, and rolls down the windows and blasts the air conditioner.

"Yeah, let's get iced coffees first."

"Of course," she turns up another favorite and we're off.

Before we change into our bathing suits, Piper makes me try on at least six different dresses to determine the best one for Saturday night. We decide the yellow sundress is the best choice. It's bright, so he will be sure to see me coming. It's sexy, because it's fitted on the top, and throughout my torso yet flirty and modest, because it flows into an A line to my knees. Perfect.

I put on my new white swimsuit; I had to save the white swimsuit for August, so it and my pasty skin tone won't blend together. I'm always tan by August, thanks to living next to the lake. The lake is a short walk from my house, across the thick green lawn, down to the wooden dock my dad built and here you are at the usually, icy water. We own a Jet Ski and float rafts for lakes but today, Pipe and I just want to lie out in the sun, read trashy magazines and gossip.

"You don't think Ryan has a girlfriend, right?" I ask, lying on my back in the lounge chair on the dock.

"No, guys don't usually want girlfriends during the summer. Who wants to start a relationship when we're all about to go off to college?"

"Um. You and Grant."

"That's different. I wouldn't call it a relationship. It's casual. We aren't boyfriend and girlfriend, like you want to be with Ryan," she counters.

"OK. I'll expect him to be single." I close my eyes and soak in the warm sun. I'll probably be sorry for this sun exposure later. Still, I can't help myself. Of course, I have an spf 15 on and an spf 30 on my face, no one wants to be red. *Ugly skin, that thought reminds me of an incident yesterday at work.* "Did I tell you that crazy guy, John "Kooky" Harper, came into the diner last night all drunk and loud, talking about some lady threatening his son?"

"What?" Piper sits up and takes off her sunglasses, "You didn't tell me." She whacks me with her magazine on my arm. The slightest societal infraction is enough fun gossip for this town. Everyone's ears perk up at abnormal behavior.

"Ow. What the heck?"

"Go on, go on." She rushes me for information. "Everything happens when I'm not there," she pouts.

"Yeah, Kooky comes in and sits at the counter saying how his son is being threatened by the Mom of a daughter, his son may or may not be seeing. The Mom said she was gonna call the cops on his kid for statutory you know what and he'd be damned if some woman was going to ruin his kid's life. Yada, Yada, Yada. He started cussing, so Mike told him he needed to get out of there 'cause he was upsetting the customers."

"Dude, he's a nut job. Did they ever find out what happened to his wife?" Piper puts her sunglasses back on and reclines once again, sated with some juicy gossip.

"No, I don't think anyone knows what happened to her. Some people think he killed her, chopped her body into tiny little pieces and fed her to the bears."

"What? No, he killed her, stuffed her and sets her out for the holidays." We both laugh at the direction our wickedly, sick minds are going.

"But honestly, I don't know what happened to her. They would fight all over town but they seemed to always make up. Maybe she left?"

"Maybe he keeps her locked in his basement," she says, sounding a little more serious, giving me chills in the heat of the afternoon.

"OK, stop. I'm getting freaked out."

"Either way," Piper continues, "that guy is a nut job."

"Agreed."

The sun starts going down and we're called for dinner.

My dad grills hamburgers, which we then throw on some bleu cheese and bacon to make it outrageous. Piper heads home because she, too, has to work tomorrow morning; although, she's working the early, early shift, 5:30 to about 10:30 in the morning.

Later that evening, Dad and I walk down to the dock and sit in the lounge chairs. I hold my teacup with both hands close to my chest; I'm not cold but it's comforting.

My dad is a funny guy. He is outgoing and friendly to everyone he encounters. Very charismatic. He caught my mom's attention with his humor. Not sure how she reeled him in because she is a super quiet and shy person. Maybe she laughed at his jokes and he couldn't look away? Dad and I have always been real close; maybe because I find him hilarious or because I'm the baby of the family. Either way, there's a strong bond there. I favor his features mostly. We both have thick brown hair, green eyes and olive skin. Mom has reddish brown hair, brown eyes, pale skin and freckles. Poor thing can never get a tan. At least I have a chance at some color. Because the grays started coming in, she dyes it blonde now.

I can listen to my dad talk for hours. He has many great stories. His parents were missionaries in Africa for many years. His time there sounds to me akin to suffering yet it wasn't to him. He was pretty young and didn't know any different. It was how they lived. Every day was an adventure. It's made him into who he is today. I enjoy our time together.

"Well, Victoria," Dad always says my full name, even though everyone else usually calls me V. "Are you excited to go to college?" He doesn't sound too excited.

"Yeah, I'm a little nervous, of course, but I think it's going to help that Piper will be there with me."

"That's why I'm nervous," he says, with a chuckle.

I laugh. "We'll be fine Dad. I think Bruce and Amanda will be over here more because of their equally empty nest. You four will be making Piper and me worry."

He laughs. "That may be true, although, Lieutenant Bruce usually has a tight leash on all of us."

"Yeah, he's a pretty controlled guy. What happened with Piper? He doesn't even have a leash on her." We both laugh again.

"Piper has always had him wrapped around her finger. Some daughters do that to their dads," he gives me a little grin. I knew I was his favorite daughter. *Eat that, Valentina.*

After a while, we sit in silence, enjoying the warm summer night and listening to the locusts. I love being able to look at all the stars and be close to the water and all the trees. This is my favorite place. I can't imagine not living here forever. Although, I haven't actually traveled the world, I've been to California, Arizona and a few other places, although nothing is the same as home. Home is Burton, Idaho. Idaho doesn't seem to get much love unless you just finished a bag of chips.

Yes, we are known for potatoes, which are, of course, associated with couches, grease and oil, scalloped, fried, baked or mashed. One time, Idaho produced 2.7 billion potatoes in a single year. Go us. Honestly though, I love being here, especially living on the lake and being able to explore the woods. It still fascinates me.

Something nasty invades my daydreaming or evening dreaming, rather.

"What's that smell?" We look around and see a glowing light off in the distance with smoke coming from it. "That smells nasty," I scrunch my nose.

"People burn their trash all the time; yeah, that stinks. Let's head inside. I want to catch the news."

Why do old people always like to watch the news? I vow to never watch the news when I'm older. It is always depressing and horrible. I don't need to hear some of the stories they play. It stays with me for weeks and ruins me. All I need to know is the weather and if there's a serial killer in my town.

I head upstairs to take a hot shower. Instead, I grab my phone, which had vibrated itself to the floor, seeing texts from my friend, Camden. Most people immediately hate her. She is a drop-dead gorgeous blonde bombshell. We've been friends since seventh grade, when she moved here from Georgia.

She was beautiful then too, all the boys wanted to ask her out and most did. Almost all the girls gave her dirty looks and were rude to her. I think many of the girls were dumped when Camden came to town, not making it any easier.

Piper and I befriended her, and she's honestly loved us ever since, very loyal that Camden. She could have dropped us after making friends when she joined the volleyball team, the tennis team, or even the French club; yet that's not Camden. She made several new friends after a while but remembered who didn't judge her in the beginning.

I open the first text.

"Guess who came into the gym today?"

A second text since I didn't respond yet.

"Maybe ur at work? Ryan MacKenna. He looks good V. I asked him if he had a lucky lady and guess what, he said 'NO'. So that's good, V."

"Call me some time, I wanna c u b4 you leave 4 college."

Camden can most certainly ask that kind of question to a guy, without fear of Ryan thinking she was hitting on him, because she is happily dating the star of the hockey team. He got a scholarship to Washington State University. That's where she is going to nursing school. It's funny, she's this beautiful dainty southern belle and she's dating a big husky brute, who has broken his nose at least three times. Not that looks matter, but it's funny to pair them up—you wouldn't put them together on your own. I text her back.

"I KNOW. Pipe told me Grant said Ryan was coming into town. But I thght it wasn't until 2mrw? Yes, let's get 2gether for lunch at Cavanaugh's next week. Thursday is my last day at work. Friday would be good. Want Piper to come too? I'll be at the bonfire this Sat. too. Thanks for the Ryan dating update. It's good to know the timing is right."

She responds quickly to my relief, because I'm exhausted.

"Absolutely, she can come. I don't know if Ryan came in early or Grant was mistaken? Whatev. Can't wait for next week! I miss you ladies. I'll see you at the bonfire."

I text her back.

"Miss you too!! Nighty nite."

I get in bed, immediately entering dreamland.

Chapter 2

Three? No. Two Is A Crowd

I awake to a sun shiny morning. I don't have to be at work until 10 o'clock so I slowly make my way downstairs. Dad is already at work and Mom is running errands. Is it strange my mom wrote a note to tell me that? Maybe she thinks I'll worry someone kidnapped her?

I eat a blueberry bagel, a banana, and down some chocolate milk. I probably won't get to eat again until I get home from work. Maybe I'll grab a yogurt to take.

I read my horoscope and head upstairs to get dressed. Apparently someone new is coming into my life today. I guess Ryan might stop by the diner?

Hmm…better put a little perfume on and make sure my makeup is perfect.

My diner uniform consists of black pants and a hot pink polo shirt. We don't have any guy waiters at the diner right now but when there are, they wear red polo shirts. If Ryan comes into the diner, there's nothing I can do about my appearance in my uniform.

The diner is about seventeen minutes from my house and right in the center of town. Main Street is made of all brick buildings. Every shop is taken, too. There aren't any vacant or boarded up shops in our town. Many tourists come eat at the diner during their stay and the locals often come for breakfast or a quick sandwich for lunch. I love seeing the different kinds of people that come through. I often see excited fathers and sons ready to go fishing or hunting, while the wives and daughters are excited to go shopping. Occasionally, I'll see a few teens who could not care less about fishing, shopping, hunting, eating, being out of bed and especially don't want to be on vacation with their parents.

There is a lot to offer for the tourists regarding antique shopping, salons and spas. We have a vintage movie theater right across the street from the diner. I love looking at it. It's beautiful. The diner is made up to look old-fashioned with black and white checkered floors and red glittery seats in metal frames. On the weekends, Mike puts on 50's music, which the tourists eat up; but frankly, for us who work here, and the regulars who come in, it gets to be too much sometimes. We begged Mike to only do it on the weekends and not every day. He happily obliged. Soft rock plays the rest of the time.

Swallowed Ashes

I once had customers who had come all the way from Vermont. I can't imagine what we have that Vermont doesn't have but they said it was warmer here and they were looking to relocate. To each his/her own. I love hearing all of their stories, some are hilarious.

I had a newlywed couple traveling through on their honeymoon. They not only got a flat tire but also had to carry all their bags because the spare tire had also blown out after he spent over an hour putting it on. They came in here right as we were about to close and they both almost went into hysterics. Mike let them in more because he was scared of an outburst rather than being kind. I helped them see the funny side of their situation and convinced them to let me take their picture, dirty, sweaty and ratty hair so they could look back on it in twenty years and laugh about it.

I try not to take advantage of the fact that Mike seems to favor me over most of the staff. I know this because he always gives me the better sections. Always. With my constant working lately though, Mike gave me Saturday off and I don't even feel bad about it. It's not too bad for the rest of the gals who have to work Saturday. Mike will be closing the diner early anyway. Everyone in this town goes to the bonfire.

"Hey, Pipe. You leaving already?" I tease her, knowing she's been here for a few hours already.

"Yeah. I am going home and passing out on my bed. I was supposed to stay until 10:30, but Mike said since you're here, I can go," she smiles.

"OK, have a good sleep."

"See ya."

I clock in, and find I'm working with Ava and Diane. Great. I'm not quite sure how Ava got this job but it sure isn't because she's on the ball. You constantly have to tell her to roll up silverware or to bus a table. She's definitely in her own world. With Diane, it's hit or miss. I can't ever gauge her mood and I usually get it wrong. I have a theory I'm testing, though. If I come in and say "Hi Diane, how are you?" and she rolls her eyes at me, I know to ignore her and stay out of her way all day; but if she actually responds with any sort of answer, I can say a few things to her throughout the day without any looks of contempt. It's busy on Fridays with the lunch crowd, people take off from work early and swing by for dinner and tourists start flooding in, as well.

I check which section I'm in and, as I'm putting on my apron, Ava asks, "V? Is douche bag one or two words?"

I look up, completely confused by her random question. I notice she is on her phone, texting. I honestly don't know, so I take a guess. She happily types away on her phone and never looks up. I head out into the dining room and try my greeting on Diane.

"I'm doing all right; but keep that Ava girl away from me. I've told Mike time and time again that girl is constantly on that device and should be fired."

I acknowledge in my mind, by device, she means cell phone. To keep on her good side for at least a few hours, I agree. "Yep. I'll try to keep her busy with rolling the silverware," I smile, grabbing the coffee pot and start pouring refills.

Lunchtime is here in no time. A few of my friends come in and are waiting to be seated. Although Diane was supposed to get the next table, I think she knew they'd be bad tippers and let them sit in my section. I've known these kids my entire life. We run with different circles of friends now but we're all still friendly with each other. I greet them and start to take their orders.

"I want the mountain goat salad but I don't want the cheese or the croutons. No onions either. Can you put the dressing on the side, too?"

I giggle as I try to keep up with her demands. Rachel is a sweet girl, a little wild but sweet. She's Korean American and has beautiful long black hair. Anytime her parents get too strict about homework, after school activities or too demanding about her social life, she threatens to cut her hair off. It has nothing to do with her culture only that her parents adore her hair. I witnessed such an incident a few months ago when they told her to be home at 9:30 p.m. after prom. Prom didn't even end until 11:00 and man did she put up a fight. Finally, she brought out the big guns and grabbed the kitchen shears. Her mother screamed in Korean at her and smacked Rachel's father with the kitchen towel. Her father finally said she could come home at midnight but no later or she'd be grounded for the entire summer. We all knew Rachel wouldn't let that happen but she got what she wanted for the moment and we happily left for prom. Long hair and all.

She hands me the menu and gives me a big cheesy smile, as if she wasn't being high maintenance. Charlie gives me his order, Taryn next. As she hands me her menu, someone from behind me

31

glides a hand across my lower back and says, "Hey," in my ear.

I blush, "Hey Matt," as I turn around to face him. I hear Rachel giggle behind me. Matt is a great guy. We dated off and on for about a year. Even went to senior prom together. I got sick of the arguing. We couldn't seem to agree on anything. We've only been broken up for a couple of months but, mentally, I've already moved on.

He squeezes between me and the table to sit down next to Rachel. He doesn't look at the menu before ordering, "I'd like steak."

I had already started writing steak before he ordered it. As I'm writing side of veggies and water, he stumps me.

"Side of veggies and a coke."

A coke? He never drinks soda. I glare at him and ask, "Since when?" No doubt he is doing this to irritate me. I take a deep breath. I don't care.

"You've missed so much. I'm not the same Matt I once was."

Charlie howls and the girls snicker. I have no idea what he is referring to, so I smile, "Neat."

I turn around and put their orders in. I bus two of my other tables so they can be used. We are so busy, I can only afford small talk with my friends. I remind myself several times why Matt and I broke up. He can be very charming. Every time I go to their table, he's flashing his beautiful smile at me. I hope they leave soon.

I'm constantly distracted by anyone opening the door, hoping it's Ryan. Someone should take that stupid bell off the door. I shouldn't assume he'd come to the diner. Why would he? I was only wishing he would come in, so I could see him.

I see my friends getting up to leave and I wave bye. I finish taking an order, turn it in and go to bus their table. I smile at the full coke Matt apparently didn't drink. Yep. He was trying to get under my skin. Matt must have been waiting by the door. He comes over and asks, "Are you going to the bonfire tomorrow?"

"Yeah, of course." I try hard not to ask but I don't want to be rude, right? "Are you?"

I keep my head down, wiping the table quickly. I organize the salt and pepper and elbow him out of the way so I can clean the seat. He grabs my arm. I stop cleaning immediately and stand up straight. I take two steps back to give myself room for clarity and so he has to release me. I look him in his brown eyes and try not to like he's grown his brown hair out a little.

"Yes, I'm going to the bonfire. I thought maybe we could hang out before we go off to college."

"I don't think that's such a good idea."

He stands there for a few seconds. He doesn't seem surprised. He was probably expecting that response. I guess he agrees. "When do you leave?"

"In about two weeks." I fidget with the towel in my hands.

"Me too."

"You're going to UCLA right?"

"Yeah. My roommate seems like a nut."

I laugh, "Why?"

"He keeps emailing me about fraternities and game schedules and bars we can't even get into yet," he laughs then sighs. I can tell he is excited to go.

"Sounds like you're going to be busy. Are your parents mad you're going so far away for college?"

"No. Well, my mom, maybe. Honestly, I think they're excited to have an excuse to visit California more often. Now they have a reason to go to the West Coast and the East Coast, whenever they want."

"Your sister still lives in Boston?"

"Yeah. She got engaged in June. I think she'll be staying there forever. The guy was born and raised there."

"Oh, I bet your mom is upset."

"Yeah, but I heard her tell my dad he better fly her out to Boston every three months or they will be packing up to move to Boston."

"Oh, boy. Ultimatums."

"You should be familiar with those."

"Shut up, Matt," I give him a fake glare and smack him in the arm.

He laughs.

At the same time Mike yells, "V," Charlie opens the door and tells Matt to hurry up. I guess our time is up. I give Mike the index finger, signaling him to give me another minute.

"It was nice catching up. Good luck in California and tell your parents I said 'hi'."

He grabs me for a hug. He says in my ear, "Have fun in Boise," he kisses my cheek gently and leaves.

I may see him at the bonfire but that was probably our last encounter and conversation until Christmas break. Wow, who knows? Maybe not until next summer even.

Mike has to yell my name one more time to bring me back from my thoughts. I jump, quickly finish cleaning the seats and move on to the next table.

Finally, my day is over. My feet are killing me and I don't think I can stand or walk anymore.

After my six-and a half-hour shift with no lunch break, I head straight home, ravenous.

Piper calls as soon as I walk in the door.

"Hey, Pipe. What's up?" Exhausted and hungry I can't manage much energy.

"You know I love you right?"

Great. I already know what she is going to say. I groan into the phone.

"Please V. Please. I'll cover two shifts next week. Please." I can imagine her big eyes and puppy face. "Grant said he'd meet me at the bonfire. So, I have to get my hair done and Marty couldn't get me in today and the only appointment available is Saturday morning."

"It's gonna be dark, he won't see your hair."

The line is silent and I know she's pouting. "Fine Pipe but you will be covering me next week. I'm serious."

"Yes. I promise. I promise."

"It better not be a 5:30 shift either."

"No it's just lunch. Ten to two. Thank you so much V. Thank you."

"You're welcome. See you tomorrow night." I throw my cell phone back into my purse and walk over to the living room window.

The living room has a huge window facing the lake. We have a wrap-around porch and it extends to a deck off the kitchen and wraps around to the living room. It's so lovely to sit out there and drink hot chocolate in the spring. There is so much wildlife. Egrets, ducks and swans swim by. I'm not much of a bird fanatic but it is beautiful to witness. The water looks very inviting, I think I'm going to go for a swim and release some tension named Piper.

"Hey, V, how was work?" my mom asks, while cutting up bread in the kitchen. I flinch, not realizing I had walked right by her earlier and didn't even know she was there.

"It was fantastic," I say, with a cheesy grin then immediately wipe the fake smile and slump onto the kitchen bar-stool.

"Do you want some iced tea?"

"Yeah." I put my head down on top of my arms.

"Just think, you won't have to work much longer and it will be school, school, school."

"Woo-hoo." I cheer sarcastically, without raising my head.

My mom sets my iced tea on the counter with a slice of buttered bread. I sit up straight and ask how her day was, trying to lighten my mood.

She had a good day at the high school. They set up their classrooms and had a staff meeting before the new school year starts. She has worked there twenty seven years teaching Math and subbing in for gym teacher and health class. She started doing part time recently, three years ago and only teaches science class for four periods. She's happy for the change in subjects. She loves doing all of the lab work and looking at things through microscopes. She rarely gets to take the students out to the woods or the lake to gather specimens. So on some weekends she and my dad go out and look for things she can use in the classroom. She loves her afternoons at home doing gardening or riding her bicycle. She also volunteers at church, to help set up and cook the free community meal on Wednesdays. She certainly keeps herself and my dad busy. She signed them both up for a mini-marathon this past spring. He went along with it but I don't think he thinks of those kinds of things on his own; but she puts their names down for all sorts of activities, including whitewater rafting, mini marathons, cooking and dancing lessons and he just goes with it.

My parents met in college, attending most of the same classes to become teachers. My mom was there on a basketball scholarship and my dad worked day and night to pay for his tuition. They both had a love of teaching, gardening and being outdoors. They hit it off immediately and spent as much time together as they could. Going on hikes, studying together and, of course, he always went to her basketball games. They waited until they graduated from college to even get engaged but married quickly after the engagement. They eventually found jobs here in this small town, my mom at the high school and my dad at the middle school. They bought this little house by the water because they both knew being close to the lake would keep them adventurous. Rowing in the lake and hiking in the woods is something they always do. Being able to add on to this house over the years, raising a family, plus working, has kept them very busy.

"Dinner is only going to take ten or fifteen minutes, so when do you want to eat?"

"When is Dad getting home?" I finish my piece of bread and down my iced tea.

"About 5:30, maybe thirty minutes," she says, after looking at the clock.

"OK. Maybe forty-five minutes. I wanna go for a quick swim." I hop off the stool, "Unless you need help."

"Oh, no V. I'm good. You go swim." She shoo's me out of the kitchen. "Dinner will be ready in forty-five minutes."

"All right." I go upstairs, jump into my bathing suit, grab my towel and head out to the dock. Our property is the only house next to the lake. The other houses in the neighborhood are across the street and spread out. It's not surprising I'm the only person out here.

I lay my towel down on the Adirondack chair, covering the faded stencil of our last name. I never dip my toe in first as many people do. I already know it's going to be cold, so why torture myself?

I jump right in. Crap, it is cold. I shiver and shake a bit then start a few laps to warm up. My mom made us take swimming lessons when we were young. She didn't want us to be afraid of water. Since then, it's always kept my interest. I love swimming; it's kind of therapeutic for me. Working at the diner can make my body ache and swimming usually works out the kinks and gets me back into shape. My body temperature now agrees with the water.

I float on my back, soaking up the hot sun. I close my eyes and daydream once again about Ryan MacKenna.

Ryan was my high school sweetheart, although he wasn't aware of it. I always had a crush on him but I could never tell him. Every time I got around him, my brain shut off and I lost all confidence. I wasn't nervous around other guys, just Ryan. I have no idea why. I've had my share of boyfriends, too. Maybe the difference is they mostly were the ones to ask me out. Ryan never did. He usually had a girlfriend anyway and it just never happened. The timing wasn't right.

I am a true believer that timing is everything. I think things happen for a reason and if you want something bad enough, at some point it will happen. So I have been patiently waiting for the right time and I'm confident this is our time.

After graduation, he went to visit family on the East Coast then he and that whole half of his family were going on vacation to...hmm...I can't remember where but I know it was a hot and sandy sort of place.

Now he is going to be at the same university Piper and I are attending. That will sure make dating easier. I've it all planned out. We'll have a class together so we'll definitely sit next to each other because we'll recognize each other from high school and, because we don't know too many people at the university, we'll be forced to spend time together. We'll fall in love and have many babies. Well, maybe two but that's negotiable.

As I continue daydreaming about whether our kids will have red hair, as he does, or brown like mine, I start to doze a little. It's so calm and quiet out here alone. The water muffles all the noises around me. The saying, "Silence is deafening," is funny when your ears are underwater where everything is completely silent but the water in your ears seems loud. I could actually be floating next to someone right now and not even know it.

Scaring myself, I open my eyes at the thought. Right then a big black bird, a crow maybe, swoops down near my face. Startled, I scream, and my head goes under without my brain truly making the decision, as I flap my arms toward my face, trying to cover it. I come up, gulping lake water. I cough violently to clear my throat and breathe. Some kind of pang hits me in the gut and I go under again, this time holding my breath. As I come back up, my head, arms, hands and fingers, legs, feet and toes are all tingling. My head spins and I feel sick. My vision is slightly blurred so I close my eyes, trying to center myself again. Still coughing and still trying to catch my breath, I open my eyes and see I'm surrounded by bushels of leaves and sticks. I swim toward the grass so I can stand up and I start pulling sticks out of my hair. As the shrubs pass by me, I see a tiny worm on one of the leaves. I stare in disbelief.

Did that worm say hello to me? I get closer and stare harder, as if willing the worm to speak again. Nothing. I roll my eyes at my moment of hysteria and dip myself back under the water, this time to rid myself, purposefully, of any more leaves and sticks. I've been trained on how to handle certain dilemmas while swimming but never one involving a bird attacking my face. I'm surprised by my reaction regarding the bird. I should definitely exhibit more control, seeing as I'm an experienced swimmer but I guess there's something to be said about the element of surprise. I never had to deal with that during swimming practice. I guess that is enough excitement for one day. Time to go inside.

"Um…hello?" I hear the meek voice again. This time it's definitely not a worm.

I look around, expecting to see someone in the water. How embarrassing. Did someone witness my brilliant reaction a moment ago? No one else is here. Where did that voice come from?

"Yeah?" I answer as I look around the lake. I look at the dock and I don't see anyone there, either. The voice sounded as if she were right next to me. "I don't see you." I whisper quietly to myself, as I swirl around in the water still seeking the source of the sound.

"That's probably because I'm in your head," the voice says, in a tone coated in 'obviously, you idiot.'

"Y-e-a-h." I pause, keeping still, yet moving my eyes while searching for someone. "OK, so I'm gonna get out of the lake now," I call out. "Yep, too much sun and not enough food," I say to myself as I swim to the dock.

"No, I'm serious. I'm in your head. Or, maybe your whole body. I can't tell," the voice mutters. Now she seems to be talking to herself. "I'm dead, and my soul chose you to...um...haunt. No, that's not the right word." She laughs. "Um...my soul chose you to help me with my unfinished business. Like you're my host." She says this as if I should be grateful for this opportunity.

"Oh, gosh. I feel a little dizzy," I moan. I get out of the lake and tilt my head to one side and start jumping. I've always found this method effective when I have water in my ears.

"You can't shake me out of your head, silly. My soul is in your body." The voice yells, saying each word deliberately.

I ignore the voice, and refuse to subject myself to this level of insanity.

I walk to the house slowly, not wanting to cause any further injury to myself. Or ourselves. I laugh; yeah, I need to go lie down.

As I enter the house, the aroma of mussels simmering in garlic and bread being toasted fill the air. It sure smells good but I need to lie down. This "soul" is giving me a headache. I do my best to talk over her talking to me and tell my mom I am going to bed.

"What about dinner?" Mom asks. "It's early." She glances at the clock and continues without giving me a chance to answer her first question. "Do you feel OK?"

"Yeah. Too much sun and I have a shift in the morning to cover for Piper." I rush the words out of my mouth while I sprint up the stairs. I can't be sure because the "soul" is still talking but I think Dad asks Mom why I'm yelling.

I jump in the shower quickly, singing loudly so I don't hear any more questions and chatter. I continue my version of "O' Beautiful" while putting on my pajamas. I wonder if I should go on one of those talent shows?

"You sound horrible."

OK, no talent show. I switch to humming to myself as she keeps telling me I have to help her.

I know how to drown her out. I put on my headphones and play loud music. I grab my nail polish and slowly and precisely apply it to my fingers and toes. I lie on my bed to let the polish dry and I close my eyes and sing in my head with the music. So far, it's worked to eliminate her voice but I think I'm getting a headache now. My nails are dry, so I turn off the music and cautiously wait for another spirit outburst.

Nothing. Thank goodness.

I turn out the light and hop into bed. It's still light outside but I try my best to fall asleep.

She starts up again.

"Hey, I need you to listen to me, please. I need your help. I don't know what is going on. All I know is I'm dead and now I'm in your body." She repeats this over and over.

I toss and turn while trying to ignore her but she is too irritating. I finally give in.

"OK," I shout.

Returning to my normal tone, I respond, "If I help you with your unfinished business, will you please let me sleep?" Why not fib? This will all be over in the morning.

"OK. Agreed," the "soul" says cheerfully. "We'll talk first thing."

"How about after breakfast? After all, I did skip dinner because of someone's constant babbling," I suggest, feeling a wee bit crazy after doing so.

"Absolutely. After breakfast. I can wait. I'm already dead," she says lightly.

I sigh.

"OK, nighty-night."

"Over and out," I say, drifting to sleep.

Chapter 3

You, Me, Us, and We...

The next morning I awake, feeling so much better. I stretch and get out of bed. Completely aware of the previous evening's episode, I call out, "Hello, little voice, good morning." Silence. Hmm. *Awesome. I'm not too surprised; I mean, really? A voice in my head? A 'soul' in my body for cryin' out loud?*

I start humming a song while I'm in the bathroom. Strange, I haven't heard it since I was little.

I walk downstairs, almost skipping in relief and help my mom with breakfast. Saturday morning pancakes. My mom has been making Saturday morning pancakes since I was little. Somehow it's never gotten old. Not sure where we got the idea but we always put peanut butter on the pancakes with syrup and not butter. I won't have them any other way.

"You seem to be feeling much better."

I think my mom states this more as a question than an observation, so I respond, "Oh, much better. I feel more like myself; and only myself." I utter the last part under my breath.

"Aren't you covering for Piper this morning?" she reminds me. Always a mom.

"Not 'till 10 o'clock, not 'till 10." Mom and I have always had a silly relationship.

There's something to be said for a good sense of humor and a dash of patience on her end. Well, maybe a heaping tablespoon of patience.

"Here, take these and go eat, so you aren't late for work." She hands me a plate with a pile of pancakes. I sit and assemble my breakfast. I look around and notice someone is missing.

I ask with a mouthful of pancakes, "Where's Dad?"

"He's already started his outside chores. He has to cut the lawn before the storm this afternoon. Oh, and move the patio furniture. Our umbrella flew away last time."

I finish breakfast, put my plate in the dishwasher and start up the stairs to get ready for work.

"Good mornin', sunshine," the cheerful "soul" sings.

"Ah," I twirl around, almost falling off the first step and scream so loudly my mom almost drops her coffee cup. Simultaneously, I hear two voices: one from my frantic mother, "What's wrong?" and the other from her...

"Whoa, don't fall off the stairs. I need you alive," she chuckles.

Swallowed Ashes

"I thought you were gone," I choke in a whisper. I glance at my mom who is standing confused and waiting for me to answer, not hearing my choked words. They both speak again.

"You said wait until..." I cut her off, while my mom is repeating, more urgently, "What's wrong?" I turn my head back toward the stairs, so my mom won't see my mouth.

"Stop talking at the same time," I say through gritted teeth. I whirl around, and my mom is looking at me as if I'm nuts.

"Huh? I can't understand you," she says, staring at me.

"Nothing. I thought I saw someone right there, but it was my shadow." I give a big cheesy smile and say, "OK, gotta go get ready." Great. Now she'll really think I'm crazy.

As I run up the stairs to my room, I say again quietly, "I thought you were gone. You didn't answer me this morning."

"You said, 'How about after breakfast?'" she mocks me in a goofy voice.

"First of all, I don't sound that way and second of all, I honestly thought you would be gone in the morning," I confess, as I put on my socks.

"Oh, right, I was 'sun-sickness.'" I imagine her throwing her hands up and doing quotation marks in the air.

"Yeah," I sigh. "You're gonna have to find someone else 'cause I have to go to work and I don't think I can be your cat's-paw." I tuck in my shirt and zip up my pants.

"Your what?"

"Your cat's-paw, your host, your whatever. Look I can't help you."

"You look. I don't know why we are together but it's for a reason and to be honest, myself, I don't know how to leave you."

"Oh, great. Lovely." I roll my eyes, feeling defeated.

What in the world is going on? Why is this happening to me? How will I be able to help her? Can you hear my thoughts? No answer.

"Hey? Can you hear my thoughts?" I repeat, but aloud this time.

"No, I don't seem to be able to hear them. I can see what your eyes look at and hear what your ears hear but not your thoughts."

Good, I thought.

I head to the bathroom and grab my toothbrush. As I grab the toothpaste, I catch sight of the toilet out of the corner of my eye, igniting a list of questions.

"Can you see me?"

"Right now? No. When you looked in the mirror, I saw you."

"So you aren't hovering outside of me? Like a ghost?" I giggle at the simple ridiculousness of this whole situation.

"Oh, no, I'm like in you."

"In me?" I say with a mouthful of toothpaste.

"The best I can explain it is my soul entered your body and I can hear and see. It seems I can only see what you see, though, like literally what your eyeballs look at. I haven't tested the hearing. Like, if there was a noise you didn't hear because you were thinking too deeply but maybe I could still hear it. I sure wish I could have tasted those pancakes; they looked amazing."

"What about touch?" I hold up my toothbrush and wiggle it in the air.

"I guess. It doesn't feel like when I was human, though."

I spit, rinse and put the toothbrush down. Without looking down, I pinch my arm.

"Uh, yeah, weirdo."

"Just checking," I say.

"What do you mean about it not feeling as when you were human?" I ask as I brush my hair and put it in a wretched ponytail that my boss makes me wear.

"I don't seem to feel physical pain but I know it stung when you pinched yourself because your insides contracted. It was like a twinge."

I think about that for a minute, trying to understand by putting it into my own words.

"So, if I burn my hand, you won't feel it directly? You'll share the pain I feel or allow myself to feel inside?" That's the best way I can explain it.

"I don't know. Go burn yourself."

I snicker at her quick wit and sarcasm. I focus on the one important question or, rather, the request that initiated all these questions. I take a deep breath.

"We need a rule."

"For what? It must be good 'cause I feel nervous."

I stare at the toilet and she starts laughing.

"No talking when I'm on the toilet and no listening." She's laughing hysterically at this point.

"And close your eyes." I picture her rolling on the ground in laughter.

"You have to close your eyes for me to close mine."

"I will. Maybe you can sing while I close my eyes and plug my ears."

"All right, boss. Whatever you say. It's not like I want to see any of that, anyway."

"OK, agreed."

I grab my keys and my purse and head out, getting in my car.

"So, what was your name again? I guess we should introduce ourselves. My name is Victoria but everyone calls me V."

"I'm Natalie. Natalie Knight, with a K. And everyone calls me Natalie," she says sarcastically.

"Natalie Knight. Nice name. You have a sunny disposition, Natalie."

"What do you mean?"

"Well, you seem OK with...uh...for being...um..." oh geez, "passed away."

"Oh, dead."

"Exactly. You seem to be OK with being dead." She said it first. "So, can I ask what happened?"

"I was murdered," she says, a little too enthusiastically.

"What?" I stop before turning over the ignition. "Murdered?"

"All I remember is walking home from my friend's house and BAM."

I jump slightly at her loud sound effect.

"Sorry. I didn't mean to scare you."

"So, you were hit in the head? Or hit by a car, or shot? What?" I resume starting the car and head toward work.

"Oh, I don't know. I remember everything going black. I saw my life, I guess, flash before my eyes. Meaning I saw my entire life. I was a cute freakin' baby by the way."

I laugh. This Natalie girl is funny.

"I was drifting toward the light but I didn't want to go. I wanted to figure out what happened to me so I, like, repelled and went the other way. I came back to my body for whatever reason but it wasn't my body anymore. It was a pile of ashes."

"Ashes? Oh that does sound suspicious."

"I don't know what happened in between. I was a little busy but being alive and human one minute and dead and a spirit over my own ashes the next doesn't seem normal. So I say, murdered."

"So you don't know why you came back to your body...well, what your soul apparently thought was your body?"

"Maybe I wasn't dead, so my soul came back to reenter my body. I don't know?"

"Why didn't you come back as a ghost?"

"And leave you out of it, eh?"

I imagine a little smirk on her face.

I ignore her remark but continue with that line of thinking. "Well, how did you pick me to be your host or whatever?"

"Oh, I didn't. I don't know how we got together. As a bodiless soul, I couldn't see or do anything. It was all feelings. Like, I knew I was back on Earth. I knew I was back with my former self, albeit ashes. It felt as though I was bound to my ashes. I don't know if I was with a bulk of the ashes or scattered. Funny, it felt like a waterbed or something and then here I am, sharing your innards."

I make a face. *That's a weird way to put it.*

"I felt that," she says dryly.

"Felt what?" I ask, looking at myself in the rearview mirror, as if I can see her, too.

"I bet you scrunched your face."

I slump back into my seat. "Oh, super," I say in a monotone. No hiding my own feelings.

"OK. Back to you moving with your ashes. That means your ashes weren't a pile on the ground. They were in motion."

"Wow, you're quick," she says, heavy on the sarcasm.

"Oh, pipe down there. I have to talk it out. I never had a problem with talking to myself in private until someone entered my body, someone who can now hear everything I say."

"All right, all right. So, yes, my ashes were moving when we got together. What to figure out next, Drew?"

"Huh?"

"Or, if you prefer, Nancy...?"

"Interesting how funny turns to annoying so quickly."

"Think of me as your annoying, yet funny, little sister."

"Oh, yay," I feign excitement. "I wasn't in the market for such. Now be quiet so I can think this through."

I think back to last night and remember she spoke to me when I was in the lake but only after I choked on some lake water, hence, the waterbed feeling that her soul aura sensed. I remember the bushel.

"Maybe you were aboard the U.S.S. Bushel."

"The what?"

"There was a bushel of leaves and sticks floating in the water next to me. I noticed it after a crow or whatever swooped down and scared me and that's when I swallowed the water."

"A bird flew at your head?"

"It must have been trying to get a worm on that leaf, but at the time I thought it was coming toward my face. When you first spoke to me, I actually thought it was the worm speaking to me."

She bursts out laughing.

"Really?" I say defensively. "It's not like that would be weird at this point." I shake my hands in front of me in an up-and-down motion, hinting at my possession. "I wonder if my mom has a number to a priest," I threaten.

"OK, I'll behave. No exorcism needed."

"Hey, what do you...I mean did you look like, anyway? I need a clearer mental picture to go with your voice."

"Imagine 38-24-36."

"What?" I choke out.

"Just kidding. I was flat and lanky. I had long red hair. I was trying to grow it to my butt but it wasn't quite there yet. It was straight as a stick, my mom would say. It was a pain to wash."

She chuckles. "With red hair, I was pale and prone to having freckles but I discovered, if I stayed out of the sun, they weren't so prominent. I was about 5-foot-5 at my last physical. I lost some muscle mass when I stopped cheerleading because I stopped working out."

"Wow, you sound like a knockout. So why did you drop out of cheerleading?"

"The drama of some of the cheerleaders— the whole idea and pressures of being perfect all the time and trying so hard to impress people. Some of it was fun, though. I loved going to all the games and having so many friends but once some of the crap started, I knew it was only going to get worse in high school. Plus, I met Andrea and she was so carefree and fun. She was pretty in her own right, too, but she didn't rub it in anyone's face or let it be something she obsessed over.

"Wait. Who's Andrea?"

"My best friend. It was her house I left the night I died."

"Oh, geez. OK. Carry on with your story."

"Anyway, Andrea and I always had such a good time hanging out, going to the hot spring and to high school games. It was different hanging out with her. I wasn't so anxious anymore."

"Did your parents like her?"

"Well, my dad lives in the city and never met her but I'm sure he got a mouthful from my mom about her."

"Your mom didn't like her?"

"Well, she did think she was funny but, of course, any trouble I got into she immediately blamed on Andrea's influence."

"Was it?"

"Probably," she giggles. "But if I'd continued with cheerleading and hanging with those girls, I would probably have been doing the same things or worse. Influence was everywhere in middle school, and I made my own decisions regarding those situations. So even if it was Andrea's idea, I still said yes, ya know?"

"That's very mature of you."

"What?"

"Taking ownership of your decisions. Most kids, even ones my age, put their tails between their legs and go along with the crowd, even if they don't want to; but you are aware of your decisions and know they weren't made because of someone else. How did you meet Andrea?"

"Let's see. We sat next to each other in health class in seventh grade. She was always cracking up the class and she made sure to embarrass the teacher as much as possible. It was a nice change, watching someone actually be herself and she was so funny. So we started hanging out a bit in school and through the summer. Eighth grade rolled around and I wanted to make a change. So I did."

"Oh. So you're an eighth-grader?"

"Was. I was going to be a freshman in about two weeks."

55

"Sorry," I say sympathetically. *I don't seem to say the right things at the right time and saying I'm sorry is about the only thing I can conjure up and I truly am sorry for her; to be taken so young, to miss out on high school, parties, love, life.*

Her excited voice startles me out of my thoughts.

"Hey, turn it up."

I turn up the volume. "You like rock, too?"

"Yeah. I can feel you like it, too." The shared feeling thing is getting creepy.

I start drumming in the air and singing loudly.

"I'll do air guitar." I laugh at the thought of a little person in my head playing air guitar. *Maybe it will be possible to coexist if we get along this way. Temporarily, of course.*

I make it to work, feeling energized thanks to our car ride concert and get ready to make some money. *I'm only here to cover the lunch shift from 10 o'clock to 2 o'clock this afternoon so I won't earn too much but enough for gas money. I have my regulars but that doesn't mean they will tip me more; it only means they won't have me running around the diner asking my boss if there is gluten in this or nuts in that and asking how many calories does the Mountain Hiker Platter actually have? The answer is usually: "Enough for the Mountain Hiker to hike it off." If you aren't a mountain hiker, I wouldn't recommend it; my boss once told me the calorie count and I almost fell over.*

"Hey, V." My boss smiles at me quickly and continues counting Suzy's drawer. Suzanne has been here for about fourteen years and now that she's a bit older, Mike pretty much keeps her as the cashier. She will sometimes come out from behind the counter to fill the patrons' coffee cups and chat with them. She's a real sweet lady. She prefers the morning shift, 5:30 to 10 o'clock, which is fine with everyone else. I can't fathom thinking at 5:30 in the morning. I tie on my apron and clock in as Suzy is clocking out.

"Bye, Suzy."

"Oh, hi, Victoria." Suzy is about the only person besides my dad to use my full first name. "Well, I'm off to go play Bunko with the girls. You have a great day, sweetie." She touches my shoulder gently and grabs her purse.

"Have fun. Don't get into any trouble." I flash her a giant smile.

She laughs because we both know Suzy will never get into any trouble. She heads out to the back exit where her car is parked.

"She seems like a nice lady," Natalie says, startling me. I grab my chest where my heart skipped a beat. How could I possibly forget she's there? But guess what? I did. "Sorry, did I scare you?"

"Yeah, I forgot you were there."

"Wow. I love you, too," she says dryly.

I roll my eyes and ignore her but kindly reply to her first comment. "She is. She's a lot nicer than Diane. I'll tell you that right now."

"What's that?"

"Ahh." I scream, as I whip myself around and come face-to-face with my boss.

"What the heck, V?" He gawks at me, apparently unaware that sneaking up behind someone can potentially scare them.

"Mike, you scared me." Breathing hard, I put my hand on my chest. I am more embarrassed he may have heard me talking to Natalie or, in his eyes, myself than because I just screamed in the diner.

"Oh. Sorry. I thought you were talking to me," he says.

"I wasn't talking." I give him a sheepish grin and walk off. OK, I have to talk more quietly, I guess.

"Hey, Jason," I say to the cook. Jason is a real sweet guy. He's one of the hardest workers I've ever seen. He mans the grill and dishes out food as fast as he can. He's never late, he never takes time off and he is never in anything less than a great mood. I have no idea how someone can be happy being so close to heat and fire all day long. God bless him, though.

"Hey, V," he smiles warmly. "Why are you scaring all of the customers?" He laughs.

"I didn't mean to. Someone should tell Mike not to sneak up on people." I flash Jason a big smile and glare at Mike.

"So, Sherlock, how are we going to find my killer?"

Without moving my lips, I say, "I don't know." I walk over to my section and place rolled-up silverware, nicely wrapped by Suzy, on my tables. Dang, I forgot to put my Chap Stick in my pocket. I make my way back to the break room. It will be a horrible day, indeed, if I don't have my Chap Stick.

"We can retrace my walk home. I remember I was walking home from Drea's house, so maybe there's evidence around the area."

"Who's Drea?"

"It's my nickname for Andrea."

"Your best friend," I recall.

"Yes," Natalie continues, "or maybe we can go to Drea's house and see if she's worried about me. Like why haven't I called or texted her? What if something's happened to Drea? What if she's being held hostage 'cause she saw me get murdered." After mention of this possibility, I get a queasy feeling.

"Stop it," I say through my teeth. "You're making me nervous."

"I am?"

"Yeah. Your anxiety is altering my emotions and causing me to be anxious. It's contagious. So cut it out."

"Sorry. I didn't know my emotions could override yours." I grab my Chap Stick and zip up my purse, throwing it back into my cubby.

"Yes, I can feel yours, and you can feel mine."

Natalie bursts out laughing.

I roll my eyes in exhaustion, but continue, ignoring that what I said may sound creepy to anyone within earshot. "I can't go to Andrea's house and start asking questions. She doesn't even know me."

"Can I make you involuntarily slap yourself? I don't think I'm able to control your body movements."

"Would you grow up, please?"

"Man up then," she shouts. "There's a spider in your hair."

I flutter my hands and shake my hair.

"It's on your face," she screams louder.

I throw my hands around and actually smack my face. Not hard, just grazed.

Natalie starts laughing hard. "How would I know if there is a spider in your hair? You actually hit yourself. I guess I do have the

59

power to control you." She continues laughing. No doubt if she were a little person inside my head, she would be rolling on the floor and crying with laughter.

"You know what? I'm not talking to you anymore," I say and walk around the corner.

"Why not?" Ava says as she walks in ten minutes late for her shift.

"Oh, not you, Ava. I was talking to myself." I can't think of a better excuse. I should have said, "just kidding," but nooo, I have to make myself look crazy.

She gives me a strange look and says, "Well, I guess it's good you won't be talking to yourself anymore." She smiles, probably out of pity. "Aloud anyway," she mumbles as she walks past me. I don't think I was supposed to hear that last part. I need to be more cautious or people will start to talk.

"Yeah. I've got too much in my, I mean, on my mind." I don't even know what I'm saying any more. I rush out of the break room before I can do any more damage.

In my best Irish accent, I say, "For cryin' out loud."

"What?"

"I need to figure out how to talk to you without moving my lips. I'm gonna look nuts and nuts means no tips."

"Well, it could be that or maybe it's because you use an Irish accent out in the open when you aren't Irish...? Could be many things."

"Oh, shut up already."

"OK, OK."

As I walk toward the front of the "house," as we waitresses call it, I glance at a few of my tables to see if I have any customers. The table seating a family of four is still waiting for their brunch and I have one new customer, a woman sitting by herself, holding a coffee cup as if it were a lifeline. I'll have to thank Mike for picking up my slack and getting her a coffee. I can't imagine that Diane helped me out. I get a sickish feeling in my stomach.

"Oh my gosh," Natalie chokes out in a tone that has me alert and edgy.

"What?" I whisper, ultra-cautious about speaking to myself aloud in public.

"That's my mom," she gasps.

CHAPTER 4

Nothing To Do Except Get To Know Each Other

I have a bundle of emotions going on right now. Because I have no emotional connection to her mother, these must all come from Natalie. Shared innards, I repeat her earlier comment.

"I've seen her in here before," I tell Natalie. Her mom looks distressed and very tired. She usually comes in here and gets food to go but today she is sitting in the booth next to the window. She puts her coffee down and clasps her hands together on the table, rubbing her thumbs together and shaking her left leg. She stares out the window and looks at everyone who passes by.

I make my way toward her when Natalie says, "What are you doing? You can't go over there."

"Why?" I am barely audible but I stop in the middle of the diner, probably looking lost.

I assume, not having a valid reason, she opts out and says, "Well, what are you going to say?"

Without responding, I simply, yet nervously, walk over to her mom.

"Can I take your order?" I ask softly, not wanting to scare her.

"Oh." She jerks her head toward me. Guess I startled her anyway. "I was hoping to see my daughter."

"Oh, crap," Natalie says, as I simultaneously say the same words in my mind.

Her mother quickly explains, "I wasn't going to order, I mean. Unless I have to, to sit here."

"You're fine, you have a coffee but you can wait to order until your daughter gets here," I allow, knowing where her daughter actually is.

"Oh, no, she's staying the weekend at her friend's house. I mean, I'm not meeting her here. I wanted to apologize to her, if I happen to run into her." She looks down and almost starts to cry. I have no idea what I'm supposed to do. What am I supposed to say?

She continues, as I'm frozen in stupidity.

"She and her friend have been together since Thursday night and I haven't spoken to her. She won't answer her phone when I call. I thought maybe if they were out and about, I could apologize to her. She wouldn't dare yell at me in public. Her father would kill her if she did that." She looks up, giving me a hopeful half-smile. "Just mother-daughter stuff."

I flinch at her seemingly harmless remark.

"Oh. Bad choice of words, Ma," Natalie tsk-tsks.

It's then I know I have to help Natalie. I may have done it anyway but seeing her mother in this kind of pain seals the deal.

"Why don't you go to her friend's house?" I ask, truly wanting to know.

"Oh, gosh, no. That would fuel her fire. I'm going to let her be. If I see her, I'll talk to her but I don't want to push it. I may try to find her at the bonfire later."

"Well, I can go to her friend's house and see if they need a ride," I offer. "You know, to check in on her. Unless she has her own car."

"V, order up," Jason shouts through the kitchen window, making me jump.

"Oh, you don't have to do that. She's only fourteen so she doesn't have a car. That's so sweet of you, though. "

"It's no problem at all."

"V, hot food," Mike yells this time.

Feeling rushed, I quickly say, "I'm sure she loves you and wouldn't want you to blame yourself for anything."

She smiles up at me.

"Would you like more coffee?"

"No, thank you," she says, eyeing my nametag, "Victoria."

I return her smile and walk away.

Although the diner is closing early in honor of the bonfire, I hurry out before Mike can ask me to stay through the dinner shift.

"It's 2:15; should I go to Andrea's house?" I quickly put my sunglasses on as the sunlight is blinding me.

"Yeah. Let's see if she knows anything without freaking her out too much. Maybe we can retrace my walk home."

"What exactly do you think we will find out from Andrea and what will we be looking for when we retrace your walk home?" I ask, honestly, as I am walking out to my car. Mike makes us park as far out in the parking lot as we can.

"Well, we need to see why Drea hasn't called my mom and asked, 'Where the heck is Natalie?' Maybe we'll find out about my death on the trail of my last walk home. Like a bloody hammer," she suggests devilishly, "or my cell phone."

"Wait, how old did your mom say you were?"

"Fourteen. You?"

"Eighteen. You had a cell phone?"

"Y-e-a-h," she says, matching my snarky tone.

"I can't believe you had a cell phone. I didn't get one until my sixteenth birthday and that's only because I got a job. My parents didn't want to make the monthly payment."

"What can I say? Your parents suck."

"Oh, you're a riot, little one," I taunt her.

"I'm only as little as you are, heifer. It's your body I'm in."

"I wish I could smack you," I say and then laugh.

"That's what everyone used to say," she snickers.

Patching my bruised ego, I add, "And a size five is small."

"Oh, I was kidding, Sparky."

Irish "For cryin' out loud."

"*Liam Neeson*," Natalie exclaims.

"What?"

"He's Irish. At least now your Irish accent comment makes sense."

I roll my eyes. "That makes no sense."

"You make no sense."

I bite my tongue because she's too quick; she'll just come back at me with some sarcastic jab and we'll never get anywhere. "OK, tell me how to get there," I say, getting into my hot car, rolling down the windows and blasting the AC.

On the way there, we discuss how in the world we are going to pull this off. "Andrea doesn't even know who I am, so why would I show up there to ask about her best friend?"

"We can say we met at the diner and I told you I was staying at Drea's this weekend," Natalie says, "and I suggested you stop by and hang out."

"No offense, but why would I hang out with a fourteen-year-old?"

"Oh, true. Um, ooh I got it." I imagine her jumping up and down as a giddy teenager.

"You can stop by because we met at the diner and I asked you to drive us to the bonfire tonight."

"I probably wouldn't do that either."

"Well, you're gonna have to pretend or do you have a better idea?" she asks, kind of snotty.

"I don't. That will work just fine."

I drive up near Andrea's house and park on the side of the road. I feel so nervous. I'm not a liar. I've never had to lie about anything before. My parents are pretty cool. They have rules and all but they let me go out during my high school years. I've never been a troublemaker. Natalie breaks through my reverie.

"Are you OK? I feel nervous."

"No…yeah, I'm fine. I mean, I'm a little nervous. This isn't something I've ever done before."

Andrea's house is a small, white two-story house, all alone out here on the town line. It could use a coat of paint and a little TLC, but it's decent. The shutters are a faded yellow but there are pretty flowers in the flower box. Natalie tells me Andrea lives here with her mom and two little brothers.

I walk up to the door and reach for the doorbell, fingers trembling.

"That doesn't work," Natalie says, scaring me.

"Oh, my gosh. You scared me to death." I grab my chest with one hand in an attempt at trying to keep my heart from coming out and with the other hand I grasp my stomach to hold tight to whatever is left to keep it from coming up.

Natalie is giggling.

"Seriously, shutty, or I'll go back to the car," I threaten.

"OK," she whispers, giggling once more before keeping quiet.

After I knock several times, the door is opened by an angry-faced person wearing pajamas and a crazy bed head.

"Oh, my," Natalie whispers. "Oops, sorry, being quiet now."

I get nervous and stammer, "Um, is…uh, is…" Pause. Pull it together, moron. "Andrea?" I question. No response. "Um, is Natalie here?"

Andrea is a cute girl, maybe five-foot-five, tanned skin and her hair is a nice maroon color. I'm sure once she combs it, it's pretty.

She gives me a long stare and then speaks, "Who's asking?"

OK. Not in a friendly mood today.

"Sorry, I didn't mean to wake you," I say, "at 2:30 in the afternoon," I add under my breath. "My name is V,…uh, Victoria, but everyone calls me V. I'm a friend of hers."

"Friend?" she interrupts. "I'm her friend; she's never mentioned you, V," she sneers my name.

"A friend of her mom's," I choke out. "Sort of. We just met at the diner. I work at the diner off Main Street," I ramble. "Anyhoo, Natalie's mom said she was staying here this weekend and asked if I could give you guys a ride to the bonfire tonight," I say, with a big smile.

Andrea stands there, measuring me. One of her brothers comes to the door and pulls on it to see who is there. Andrea shoves him back and closes the door as far as it will go without smushing herself. "Aidan. Get out of here."

"I want to see who it is."

"None of your business. If you don't get out of here, I'm going to take your *T. rex* and throw it into the lake."

"Mommm." Aidan screams and I hear him run off. Andrea laughs and turns her face back toward me, while wiping her smile off it.

"What do you want?"

Did you kill Natalie? Do you know who killed Natalie? Several things pass through my mind before I can actually remember what I was saying before Aidan interrupted.

"Is Natalie here because her mom wants me to check on her and do you still need a ride to the bonfire?"

"Well, she just stepped out," she lies after a long pause.

Does she think she's somehow protecting Natalie because she doesn't want her to get in trouble for something or is she hiding something, like a murder?

"And you're about seven hours early."

"Call her Drea. That's what I call her. Maybe she'll be friendlier," Natalie recommends.

"Pick us up at 9:30," she says and starts to shut the door.

"OK. Thanks, Drea." Her head snaps up. "See you." I wave.

I start walking toward my car. "Your nickname caught her attention."

"I figured it would. No one else calls her that. My mom tried once but we made fun of her for doing it. It sounded weird coming from her."

"You never told me your mom's name."

"Oh. Her name is Kandi, but with a K ending in an i."

"Sweet." No pun intended.

I start to drive off when Natalie asks, "What is that smell?"

Hmm, *I didn't know she could smell, too.*

"What?"

"Dude, you stink."

"What? What do you mean I stink?" I sniff my shirt.

"I can only smell what you smell but since you sniffed your shirt, you definitely smell like bacon." She laughs. "I wanted you to go take a dip in the hot spring over there." I imagine that she is pointing. Realizing I have no idea which direction she means, she adds, "Like fifty yards to your right." She sounds exasperated because she has to explain.

"What about walking your path?" I ask, driving off the road a little bit so I can pull over.

"We can do that afterward. It'll just be for a minute. I wanna brainstorm about what we're gonna be doing. Plus, my shoulders, I mean your shoulders are all tight and the hot water will help loosen them up."

"How do you know my shoulders are tight?" I ask, not even aware they are until she mentioned it.

"It's super tense in that area. I figured you're sore or something."

"I'm always sore. OK, we do have seven hours apparently." I put the car into park and get out, listening to Natalie's directions on how to proceed to this hot spring place.

"Is this a part of Drea's property?" I ask, wondering if someone will come out and shoot us.

"No, but it must be someone's, otherwise more people would come here. A few of us sneak here sometimes but usually I'm too scared to come. It's terrifying at night."

We reach the hot spring, and I decide to strip only to my bra and underwear; it's still daylight, and I'm nervous that someone else will trespass.

It's hot outside for a dip into a hot spring but this will definitely relieve some stress. No matter, summer or winter, I usually take a hot shower to ease my tense shoulders. Some people have stress affecting their stomachs or they have headaches but my stress goes straight to my shoulders and hot water always helps.

I ease in, toes, feet, ankles, knees, until I'm waist deep. That's as deep as it gets so I slowly squat down until my shoulders are under the water. Wow. It feels so good, even in the heat of the afternoon. We both stay quiet for a while, enjoying the moment.

"I feel much better. Do I still smell?" I ask, laughing. She laughs, too, but doesn't answer my question.

"Hey, what would happen if you gulped down some hot spring water? Would we welcome another soul?"

"Ha. Three's a crowd, sweetheart." We both laugh at the thought but I seriously start to wonder if it could happen. I press my lips closed. I'm swirling my arms in the warm water and think to ask why Natalie wanted to come here.

"So, you came here with Drea often?"

"Yeah," she replies, but I can feel she is withholding something. "Drea's mom told her about this place years ago," she continues. "They came here together a few times but now Drea has a boyfriend so they come here together."

"Who's her boyfriend?" Not that I would know who he is but I ask out of a natural instinct.

"This week?" she giggles. "His name is Robbie. Robbie Stewart. He's like seventeen."

"Robbie Stewart? I know him," I say. I am shocked; one, because I actually know him; two, because a seventeen-year-old is going out with a fourteen-year-old. That is disturbing.

"How old is Andrea?" I ask judgmentally.

"She just turned fifteen." Natalie can sense my disapproval and says, "He got held back in fifth grade, so he's a junior this year. And we're freshmen. Oh, well, I was going to be a freshman."

"This may sound like a stupid question but are you sad to be dead? I mean, you seem to have a sense of humor about it all."

"There's nothing I can do about it. I know I'm dead. Nothing I can do will change that. So maybe that makes me find humor in it. I'm just going with it. This is how it is. You and me and sunny dispositions. Maybe I have the choice to be a demon and haunt people but maybe I don't."

"I'm glad you're not a demon. This would be a whole different story," I say, and we both laugh.

The clouds start rolling in and I can see lightning off in the distance.

"Better get out," I say and start putting my clothes back on. *I hate having wet undergarments but what are you gonna do, ya know?* Before I can finish putting on my shoes, it starts raining. "Dang." As I quickly lace up my work shoes, the soft patter of the rain grows into a downpour.

"Hey, go left. There's a cave over there," Natalie shouts. I run to the left and can barely see anything through the thick sheet of rain. There's a stone wall. "Oh, maybe it's on the right?" Natalie says. So I run in the other direction and see a dark hole in a huge rock. It's a little cave, but shelter, nonetheless.

Now I'm completely soaked.

Thunder crashes so loud that I scream, "Good grief. That was loud."

As we sit in the little cave and wait for the heavy rain to slow, we continue talking and getting to know each other. I take my clothes off again and wring water out of my socks and shirt.

"Did you have a boyfriend, Natalie?"

I feel a spasm in my stomach. *Butterflies?*

"Kind of. We were getting to know each other. He's friends with Robbie, actually."

Again I feel she is leaving something out.

"Was anyone jealous of that?" I question.

"What do you mean? Of me and Ben?" she says, finally telling me his name.

"Yeah, was anyone jealous of you and Ben and maybe wanted to hurt you?"

"Not that I know of or knew of. That's a good road to go down. Ben will be at the bonfire tonight and we can see if any girls are hanging around him."

Swallowed Ashes

I feel another twinge in my stomach. "That scenario pisses me off, actually."

Hmm, tough to tell the difference between butterflies and knots. Both are anxious feelings.

"We were gonna be there together," she says wistfully. Her voice sounds so sad and disappointed that my enthusiasm for figuring this out plummets. "I wonder if he's called me?" she whispers, almost as if she's forgotten I can hear her.

"Don't worry; it's probably not that scenario. Just trying to talk it out, you know; just looking at our options to see if we can figure it out a little so we're not blindsided and, of course, he's called you, probably five hundred times."

I don't want to upset Natalie with the thought of jealousy. Neither of us knows, if at any moment, she could, I don't know, turn evil. The idea scares me because I would obviously be the one out of control and the host of it all. So I change the direction of the conversation. "If they don't cover the bonfire wood then, with this rain, there won't be any bonfire and we'll have to figure something else out."

"Do you have a boyfriend, V?" she asks in a silly voice. Her mood seems to be back to normal.

"Well, no. I used to until a few months ago. I seem to fall pretty quickly for guys but that's probably because of the hormones. When that dust settles, my eyes open."

"What happened with your last boyfriend?"

"I broke up with him because we didn't get along. There were good times, of course; that's why we dated off and on for a year but it was like every time things were going good for a while, there had to be a fight about something. Anything and everything. It

75

got old. He's a great guy and I wish him well but we were not meant to be."

"Aw. That sucks."

"Yeah. A few guys before that were deadbeats. I dated one guy for like a weekend then I called it off. We went to the movies and I had to pay for both of us. I thought, OK, that's fine. He'll probably pay for the ice cream after. Well, no, he didn't and when I dropped him off at his house, he asked me for gas money. I'm the one who drove. I couldn't believe it. He knew he had crossed a line. Thank goodness he was already out of the car because I drove off." I keep going, all revved up now. "It's pretty hard nowadays to find a guy who isn't a bum. I've had too many dates where the guy is obnoxious and unmotivated. Ugh. I need to date an older guy." I sigh.

She snorts, stifling a laugh, I assume. "Glad you said that, though. The part about an older guy."

"That's like the third time you've said something, and it feels like you're leaving stuff out."

Guess she didn't realize I had noticed she is keeping things from me.

"Oh," is all she says.

"Yeah, shared innards, remember?" Wow. Was that only this morning? "I can feel you're not telling me something. Obviously, Ben is an older guy?"

"Yes. He turned eighteen a few weeks ago."

"And you're fourteen."

"I was fourteen, yes. It's a small town, and we were going to be in the same high school, only a few grades apart. I was about to turn fifteen, anyway. It's not a big deal if you look at the big picture. Can you see yourself dating a twenty-two-year-old?"

"Maybe."

"Well, see, that's four years away from your age and Ben and I are, I mean were, only three years apart. It's not a big deal," she repeats, more quietly this time.

"When is your birthday?" I ask, solemnly.

"August 20th. I was going to go to dinner in the city with my dad and brother. They have a few nice restaurants there. My brother was going to take me school shopping."

I didn't know she had a brother. I can feel the sadness she feels at the thought of those plans never happening. "I'm sorry, Natalie."

She remains quiet, too many high emotions in the past few minutes to say anything, maybe.

The rain keeps tricking me. It starts to dissipate so I think I can make a run for it to my car but then it starts back up in full force. I love the smell of rain. How does rain have its own scent?

"Hey, V? What were your high school years like?"

"Well, they weren't the best years. Sometimes lonely, sometimes crowded, if that makes sense. There was never a great balance but, all in all, it wasn't too bad. I'm going to miss going to football games, hockey games and track meets. I'm going to miss my swim team and the girls on my volleyball team but I'll have great experiences at college."

"What college are you going to?"

"Boise State, baby."

"Oh, cool. That's where my brother wanted to go."

"How old is your brother?"

"He's gonna be a sophomore this year at Idaho State. Do you have a brother?"

"Yeah, Vincent. He's in the Navy and I have a sister, Valentina. She did community college for like two years. She finally went off to college last year."

"Oh, wow, your parents like that letter, huh?"

"Yeah. My dad's name is Vincent, so that's probably how it got started. My last name begins with V, too, so who knows."

"What's your last name?"

"Vigna."

"Vig-nuh?"

"Yeah."

"Oh. I've never heard of that last name before."

"Yeah, not too many Italians in Idaho." We both laugh.

"V, did you ever go to a prom?"

"Yeah. Not my freshman year, though. I had a horrible sinus infection and couldn't get better in time to go but the other three years I did."

"Did you go with a boyfriend or friends?"

"Um, my sophomore year I went with a guy friend. My junior year was with a boyfriend and my senior year was with a boyfriend. Not the same ones, though, and they didn't stick."

"Well, don't you worry. There's plenty more out there waiting to meet you."

I smile, knowing there's only one.

Finally the afternoon storm passes by. I put my damp clothes back on and I slosh my way back to the street. We need to start our search down her final path.

"I bet any evidence is washed away now."

"Maybe your phone is still there," I say with hope.

I start walking up a hill and my eyes scour the area as best as they can. There is no sign of her phone, not even in scattered pieces. No shreds of clothing, purse, lip gloss, nothing.

"No luck, Natalie. Maybe at the bonfire we'll see someone who knows something but I don't know how to go around asking people about you without raising too many flags."

The remaining clouds are dispersing and rolling away, letting rays from the sun peak through. A bright rainbow is stretching across the sky.

"That's so beautiful," Natalie gasps.

"Yeah. It looks fake, actually. I've never seen one so bright before."

"Hey, V?"

Natalie is making me feel nervous. "What's up?"

"If there's ever a time when we aren't together anymore," she hesitates, "will you think of me when you see a rainbow?"

I wait a moment to see if she throws in a "Just kidding." But it doesn't come.

"Of course, Natalie. I'll never forget you." We stare at the rainbow in silence. I can't believe it's been almost twenty-four hours since Natalie and I got together and probably about eight hours since I actually acknowledged her presence in my body. I feel so close to her already.

"The way things are going, we may be together for a long time. You may not get any action in the next few years; no guy is going to stay with a girl who tells herself to shut up or stop talking so much." *She's back. I knew she couldn't stay in that mushy moment for long.*

"You're a nut, Natalie. Let's go get ready for the bonfire."

As I'm walking to the car, I see something glistening in the mud.

"Oh, what's that?" I whisper.

I hear what sounds like a truck coming up the hill but I don't look up, as I'm so anxious to see what is in the mud. I bend down to pick it up. It's a beautiful diamond earring. I rub it a little to get some of the mud off and hold it up to examine it. My stomach instantly feels queasy and I know we've found evidence.

"That's mine," Natalie whispers.

Chapter 5

Most Eventful Bonfire I've Ever Been To

An overwhelming flood of emotion washes over me. The earring must hold a special place in Natalie's heart.

"Well, we didn't find a bloody hammer but at least the earring means your body was once in this general area, just like you thought it was."

"Yeah. I wish there was more evidence, like at least half of my body or something."

"Yeah, that would be helpful. Where did you get such a stunning diamond?" I put the earring in my pocket and brush my hands on my pants to get rid of some of the mud.

"My dad gave it to me for Christmas. It was a pity gift," she adds lightly.

"What do you mean?"

"He was trying to say, 'I'm sorry for not being around lately...and that I divorced your mother," she says, mockingly, in a tone I assume she wants to sound like her dad's.

"Oh. That's rough."

"Whatev. I don't know if it's actually a pity gift but the earrings are very pretty. I was thrilled to get them."

"Did your parents recently divorce?"

"Yep. Last summer they split up. My dad was married to his work in the city and my mom was sick of being left behind. So she cut him loose and he didn't argue."

Simple as that. Natalie makes everything so...what's the word I'm trying to think of? Nonchalant. I would be a wreck if my parents got divorced. Even now at eighteen.

"All right, what do you say we go get ready for the bonfire then come back to get Andrea?"

"Sounds like a plan. What should I wear?" For a split second I actually think she is serious. We both laugh. Natalie is such a funny gal.

Back home, I say "hi" to my own parents who are getting dressed for the bonfire. They usually go at the beginning to grab a bite to eat with their friends but then start heading out with the rest of the adults because that's when the teenagers start crowding into every possible square inch.

I grab a drink and head upstairs to my room to check my e-mail. Nothing important. I download a new song I heard on the radio and turn up the volume. I can't seem to do anything without music. It sets the mood.

"You have quite an array of tastes going on here."

"What?" I ask defensively.

"A pink-flowered wall painting-,"

I interrupt to clarify. "Cherry blossoms," I say. My eyes start scanning my room, trying to imagine looking at it through someone else's eyes.

"Yeah. Like I said, pink flowers, Incubus posters, and is that a picture of your brother in the Navy?"

"Yes, it sure is."

"A wooden dollhouse?"

"My grandma and I made that when I was little…" I don't dare tell her I sometimes imagine it being my house, envisioning myself there with Ryan and having family and friends over to visit.

"And what are all of those medals and trophies for?"

"Um." I point to the bottom shelf: "Volleyball, all four years of high school. These are from softball from middle school." I point to the top shelf: "And all of those are for swimming."

"Wow. Impressive. I'm going to guess your favorite color is orange?"

I laugh as I stare around my room. Clearly there's not a speck of orange in here but lots and lots of navy blue and red. I guess my room does look crazy: pink flowers, old trophies, random posters and bedding and décor all in navy blue and red. There are pictures of friends in frames across my entire dresser and on boards along my walls. Everything looks quite cluttered. Yeah, maybe I need a little help in the decorating area.

"So what does your room look like?" I ask, a little annoyed.

"My dad's friend is an interior decorator," she says and I roll my eyes. "So they had her do our entire house. My room ended up being pretty girly. It was done about eight years ago, though. So last year I told my dad I wanted to change it. My mom had a lot of say in it, of course, but we all finally agreed on a dark purple and white pin-striped look. Very fine stripes, though, not thick ones. I was only allowed to have like two wall photos of family and such, no other decorations."

"Aw, I would have fought my mom about that."

"Oh, no, it wasn't her fault. The decorator insisted on it." She laughs.

I take a shower and shave my legs. I have to wash my hair again. I washed it last night but with the rain soaking it and turning it into a frizzy mess, I have no other choice. I brush my teeth, comb my hair and blow-dry it straight. Then I decide I should curl it a little. I put my deodorant on and I'm about to walk out to get dressed when Natalie interrupts my routine.

"What the heck did you just do?"

"What?" I ask, honestly baffled.

"Did you swipe deodorant under your boobs?"

I totally forgot she was watching. It's something I've done for years, especially before a volleyball game but I guess I've never done it in front of anyone before.

"Yeah."

"Why the heck did you do that?"

"Well, it's hot outside and sometimes I get boob sweat."

"Boob sweat," she yells, laughing at the same time.

For some reason I don't even feel ashamed or embarrassed she is blatantly making fun of me. It's a brilliant idea.

"Yes, boob sweat." I turn on my condescending tone and explain, "When you grow up to be a big girl, sometimes you sweat in places you don't want to and deodorant helps."

"Would you use it if you had butt sweat?" she says and tries to hold her laugh so it comes out as a spitting, choking sound.

"You're acting like a child," I scream, as I walk to my room.

Thank goodness I put my robe on. Dad startles me as he calls from downstairs, "Are you OK?"

"Yes. Just yelling at the TV. Stupid reality show." No doubt my parents will talk on their way to the bonfire about my recent weird behavior.

"Uh, OK. We're leaving for the bonfire. Do you want a ride?"

"No, Dad, I'm taking my car. It's too early to go, anyway. My friends aren't going to be there until later."

"OK. Drive carefully." My dad always says this to me. Always.

"OK. You, too."

I turn off the radio and lie on my bed. I tell Natalie to zip it for a while. I need some peace and quiet. Remarkably she agrees.

85

All thoughts pass as clouds in my mind. I doze off.

A short while later, my eyes slowly open. I get up, feeling refreshed and start to get dressed. I have such high hopes for tonight. *This could be the start of the rest of my life with Ryan. I look good, I feel good, and I'm turning on the charm.*

"Fancy dress, V."

"Do you like it? Do I look stupid? I should wear the pink one, right?" I go to grab the pink dress.

"Chill. You look fabulous. Who are you getting all dressed up for?"

I can imagine the sly smile on her face. I guess we never got around to talking about my long-standing crush on Ryan.

"Oh, gosh. Are you getting nervous, V?"

I start blushing.

"Would you cut it out?" I chide her. I go to the bathroom to put on my makeup.

"Who is it?"

"His name is Ryan and tonight I'm going to ask him out."

"Wow. Ryan and V sittin' in a tree..."

I cut her off. "Would you grow up, please?"

"I can't." I imagine her sticking her tongue out at me. "How long have you known him?"

"Since fourth grade. That's when his family moved here. I've liked him since tenth grade when we had chemistry together."

"Chemistry, huh? Funny class to fall in love in."

"Yeah, we have good chemistry; the timing was never right, though. He had a girlfriend at the time and, when he didn't, I had a boyfriend. We've never told each other how we feel but there seems to be something there. Well, at least on my end and tonight I'm going to walk up to him and ask him out."

"Isn't the end of summer a bad time to start dating someone? You know? Before you go off to college and all?"

"Oh, we got accepted to the same school. Don't you worry, Natalie; I've got it all planned out."

I smile in the mirror as if I can see Natalie. I finish putting my lip gloss on and I grab my shawl. Now we're off to pick up Andrea.

We pull up to Andrea's house for the second time today. "Natalie, stay in the car," I joke.

"Ha," she giggles. "Now that is actually funny, V. I clearly have an effect on you."

"Is it creepy to say you're growing in me, I mean on me."

"Ew, you make me sound like a fungus," Natalie giggles.

I am pretty nervous about picking up Andrea. It's going to be awkward, of course, but I have to suck it up and do this for Natalie.

Andrea opens the door. She looks a heck of a lot better than she did this afternoon. Her maroon hair is styled in long lovely waves; she has a natural look yet she definitely has makeup on and she's wearing tight black pants and an off-the-shoulder black shirt with holes in it. It doesn't look trashy, though. Somehow she may be the only one who can pull it off.

"You look nice."

She ignores my compliment and starts heading to the car.

"Is Natalie coming?"

Andrea furrows her brows. "No, she's meeting us there. She's with her boyfriend."

Obviously, that's not true, but it's like Andrea believes Natalie is with Ben. Her answer has a twinge of hope. I cross her off my murderer list, which is already short enough.

"Ben, right?" I notice she only nods. "I think Natalie's mom mentioned him," I lied. "Do you like him? I mean, is he a nice guy?"

"Yeah."

Ugh. Teenagers and their one-word answers. We get in the car, and she immediately starts touching the radio. "I hope he's not like his dad, Kooky."

My brain registers this bit of information.

"His dad is John Harper?" *I'm blindsided by this newfound fact.* "That would have been nice to know," I yell into the rearview mirror, not caring if Andrea is giving me a crazy glare.

"Y-e-a-h," she starts slowly. "Ben gets pissed when we call his dad, Kooky. Ben's all right though. He's head over heels for Nat. They need to be more careful, like Robbie and me."

I can only speculate as to what she means by careful, since she doesn't elaborate. I'm going to go with 'not getting caught by adults'.

"Oh. How long have you two been dating?"

"I don't know about dating," she snickers, "but maybe five weeks."

"Oh." I leave it at that, not wanting to pry.

Heavy on the sarcasm, the rest of the car ride to the bonfire isn't awkward at all. It's peachy. As soon as we're parked, Andrea hops out and says, "Don't worry. I'll find a ride home." She disappears into the crowd of townspeople.

I stay in the car, free of eyes and ears hearing me talk to the little voice in my head. "Um, yeah, so why didn't you tell me Kooky is Ben's father?" I don't pause to let her answer. "Ben Harper. I know who he is. I've never spoken to him but I know of him. Why didn't you tell me?"

"Why does it matter?" she says naively.

"Because Kooky has a bad reputation and possibly murdered his wife," I tell her, becoming frantic at the thought. "He probably killed you, too."

"Oh, cut it out," she chides. "Ben told me his mom left both of them because she didn't want to be a wife and mother anymore. She especially didn't want to fight with John every day. She loved Ben but she wanted to explore the world and couldn't do that with him tagging along."

"Ouch." I let that sink in for a minute. "You believe Ben? That his mother just left? That his dad didn't murder her?" I ask with honest curiosity, no malice.

"Of course, I believe him." I can feel she does.

"Well, until we find your killer, I'm putting Kooky on my list."

"That's fine. It only benefits me, right?"

"Of course. All right, you ready to investigate?"

"Heck, yeah," she blurts out with enthusiasm. "You need to call on your inner Nancy Drew."

"My inner's phone is busy with you on the line." We laugh.

"OK, seriously, what's our plan?" *I imagine her wearing a black pencil skirt with a white blouse*

89

tucked in, her hair pulled back with a pencil and her notebook and pen in hand or is it a tape recorder these days? My knowledge of detectives is dusty.

"Well, let's question a few of Ben's friends and maybe even a few of yours. There must be an eyewitness, or maybe the murderer told someone they were angry with you or something?"

"Don't take this the wrong way, but I have no other way to say it."

"Go ahead."

"What makes you think anyone is going to talk to you?"

I consider this for a minute. "Charm."

"Huh?"

"Yeah, charm. Ben's friends may know of me because we're closer in age and grade level and they may be inclined to talk, if I flirt," I say, simply. "As for any girls you know, they will be much harder to talk to unless I compliment them first."

"Why?"

"Take Andrea, for instance. She was giving me the dirtiest of looks when I got to her house because she didn't know me. Haven't you seen the movie, 'Mean Girls'?"

"Yeah."

"Girls don't like new girls. They're always threatened, so if I start out, 'Omigosh, I love your skirt. Hey, I'm looking for Natalie Knight, have you heard from her?' they'll be more willing to talk."

"What if they ask why you're looking for me?"

"I can say I have something of yours or I need to give you something you left at the diner or simply that your mom is worried about you."

"OK, that's believable. What have we got to lose? We may get a few crazy looks from strangers you will probably never see again because you're leaving for college but I think this is brilliant and we should go before our nerves fry," she urges.

"Absolutely. Let's get something straight, though. I don't want to be talking to you aloud while I walk around here, so you direct me where I should go and give me names and stuff and I'll like nod or blink an eye. Can you see if I blink?" I stare into the rearview mirror, as if I am looking into her eyes and waiting for a response.

"Yeah. It's like I'm looking through your eyes. When you blink, I blink, ya know?"

I wink.

The bonfire is a community event with a few vendors and food huts, mostly so people can socialize. It's almost like a state park. There are bathrooms and sinks and picnic tables and gazebos. Other festivals, auctions and events are held here. There's a yearly kids' fest, too. *I remember going to it throughout my childhood. It was fun. Bouncy houses, a petting zoo, face painting and I can vividly remember hotdogs. Lots of hot dogs. When I got into my preteens and didn't want to come here for the kids' fest because I'd grown into an "adult," my mom made me help her at the hotdog stand, for which, of course, she volunteered.*

The bonfire, similarly, is a chance for parents to hang out and eat good unhealthy food. The kids get cotton candy and, of course, the teenagers go on first dates and gossip. It's a fun annual event but the mayor is working on attracting the carnival to come to town. That way we'll have rides and more vendors. I've always loved carnival rides.

I see a few of my friends huddled at a cotton candy machine. Camden waves at me. I wave back and make my way toward them. As my eyes are scanning the crowd, I see a familiar face.

"My mom. Hide," Natalie shouts.

Oh, gosh. I dart behind a hotdog hut sign in hopes she won't notice me. *In case she remembers me and I'm sure she will, I don't want to have a conversation with her, right now, especially because I didn't bring Natalie as she may be hoping I did.*

I watch as she walks past me. Kandi seems to be looking for Natalie and this breaks my heart. I would love to tell her the truth but I still want to help Natalie figure it all out.

"She looks miserable."

"Of course, she does. She hasn't heard from you since Thursday."

"I hope she doesn't corner Ben," Natalie says.

"Yeah," I whisper. I step back onto the path when the coast is clear and head toward my friends again.

"Hey, Camden, how are you?"

"What the heck was that?"

"What?"

"Did you hide behind that booth?"

"Oh." Dang, I didn't know she was still watching. I think quickly. "Wedgie," I say.

"Oh," she says allowing this explanation. "Did Piper find you?"

"No, why?"

"She was looking for you and said she called you and I quote, "a million times." She said it was important."

"Oh?" I say, surprised. I have no idea what Piper could want. "I left my phone in the car. Maybe I'll see her here."

I buy a water and head over to say "hi" to a few of my other friends. Then I give an excuse that I need to go get my phone so I can secretly search for Ben and his friends. Without looking, I turn from the group and walk right into a girl.

"Omigosh," I shout. "I'm sorry."

"No, it's all right."

"Hey, that's Macyn," Natalie shouts.

Not wanting to speak to Natalie aloud, I blink one eye so she knows I heard her. I take the initiative and ask, "Hey you're friends with Natalie, right?" I take a few steps around her to distance myself from my friends' earshot.

"Um, Natalie Knight?" She looks at me questioningly.

"Yeah," so I add, "you look about her age."

"Yeah, we're friends."

"I was helping her mom out by asking around. You see they got in a fight and Natalie is staying at Andrea's house. I want to try to convince her to talk to her mom. She's worried. Have you heard anything or seen Ben?"

Macyn stands there a little, bewildered.

"Compliment," Natalie reminds me.

"Cute shirt by the way," I observe and smile big.

"Thanks. I thought it was nice but not too nice to wear to the bonfire."

"Totally," I say.

"Ben was in line for a pop and I asked him if Natalie was coming. He said she was supposed to meet him here but he hadn't found her yet."

"Aw. He was looking for me, V." Natalie murmurs.

"Oh, cool. Thanks, Macyn." I turn and walk off immediately, remembering she hadn't told me her name.

Looking around, I see the gypsy tent. It's a little different this year. Usually there's a clear magic ball out front with a sign that says, Palm Readings. Now there is a sign that says Medium and Psychic Readings. I guess I don't have time for that silly indulgence this year.

I start to walk by as someone calls out, "Victoria?"

I turn to see who it is. It's an old woman who is, no doubt, the new resident of this gypsy tent. She is wearing the normal costume: flowing dress and belt with a head wrap over long flowing hair. I expect the tresses to be gray but she must dye it brown. I've actually never seen so many bangles on one person before but, with the whole getup, it works.

"Yes?" I have no idea how she knows my name so I can't answer her without making it a question.

"Dude, how does she know your name?"

For obvious reasons, I ignore Natalie's question.

"I've been waiting for you all night," the woman says.

"Me? Why?"

"You have something very special happening to you. I want to help."

"Whaaatt?" Natalie says what I'm too stunned to say.

All I can do is stand there with my mouth gaping open. What can I say anyway? How does she know what's happening to me? Maybe she says that to everyone passing by. I'm obviously paranoid.

My subconscious reminds me of the main question: How does she know my name?

"Please come in."

The gypsy knows my name and invites me in, of course, I go in. I have to see what this is all about.

The tent is pretty dark, although there are candles in the center of her small round table. There are three chairs so I sit on the one closest to me.

There are little trinkets hanging off the tent. I'm not sure what any of them are. Some are shapes and others have stones within the shapes.

I suddenly remember I have to pay to have a reading. I open my purse and pull out a few loose bills. I come up with ten dollars.

"Are you going to ask this broad what's going on, or should I?"

I roll my eyes. "So what's this about something happening to me?"

The woman sips her tea and takes a seat across from me.

"It seems you are experiencing medium-like behavior."

"What do you mean?"

"Well, I'm a medium. I can communicate with the deceased. I can sense you can, too. I know one of my own when I see them."

How? Maybe she saw me talking to Natalie? But one would assume I was talking to myself. I don't respond to her. I don't want to admit aloud my body has been taken over by a fourteen-year-old dead girl.

She smiles at my hesitation. "You don't have to answer. I already know."

"You didn't ask a question," I state flatly.

"I understand you aren't ready to talk about it but let me tell you, being able to communicate with the deceased is a blessing. It's a service to those who didn't get to say good-bye to their loved ones and for the living to do the same. It can be a wonderful experience if you let it be. The spirit I see around you is in need of serious help."

"I think she means the spirit in you," Natalie chimes in.

The woman continues, not knowing she was interrupted. "She's a funny and feisty one, isn't she? Those are always a pleasure to work with. She needs your help to find answers. You are together for a reason you don't understand yet. As much as this is her journey, it is your journey, too, Victoria. I hope you decide to embrace it. She's very fixed on you. I can't get a clear reading on her. I know she's there but for some reason I can't hear her. It's very confusing."

Before I can stop myself, I blurt out, "She's trapped."

The gypsy's eyes widen. "Are you talking about possession?"

I nod my head.

"Oh, my. Well, that explains quite a few things."

"Like what?"

"For one thing, I can't see her. I usually see the spirits but I can't see this one. I know she is there, though. It's like I feel her presence, her personality, but I can't hear her."

I ask her a question I have been wondering about off and on.

"What happens if I can't help her? Will she stay forever?"

"I see success as an outcome. You need to be strong and courageous enough for it."

A few giggling girls walk in, not knowing we are in the middle of something. They apologize and step back out. I stand up and hand her the money.

"I didn't really give you a reading. Only encouragement."

I place the money on the table. "Tell me something then."

She closes her eyes and inhales deeply. After a few breaths, she opens her eyes.

"Your GrandPappy says change your major."

I try not to show any emotion. That's exactly what I called my mom's dad. GrandPappy.

She smiles at me. "And I see a handsome man who will love you with all his heart. He is a servant to people in his own way." She shivers. "Very handsome. Tall with dark hair."

I laugh. She is obviously seeing the wrong person or my brother. Gross.

I turn to leave but remember one more question...

"How do you know my name?"

She puts the money in her bra and replies, "You waited on me yesterday at the diner."

I'm not prepared for such a natural, non-magical response. Embarrassed, I turn and retreat quickly. *She must not have been wearing all that attire. She probably dressed like a normal adult. I don't remember her at all.*

Natalie is laughing hysterically. I am so disoriented, I don't even know where to walk. I stop

97

near a cotton candy booth and sit on someone's ice chest. I close my eyes and try to re-center myself.

"That was crazy, V. I totally believe her, though. I wish she could have given me my cause of death or something. Anything to help us go in the right direction."

"Yeah," I say with my eyes still shut. "Let's just forget any of that happening right now and tell me what I'm supposed to do again. My brain is completely fried."

"Um. We were going to look for Ben or his friends. Maybe see if anyone has heard anything about me. Still not sure how we are going to do that, though. Maybe as soon as you bring up my name, someone will have a reaction that is suspicious and we can go from there."

"OK." I take a deep breath, open my eyes and stand up slowly.

As we're looking around, Natalie spots a few more people she knows; Ben's best friend Tyler, *aka* "Slim", which is funny because he's rather husky; a tall skinny kid named Robbie, who is apparently Andrea's beau and a guy I actually know, Justin, who is of medium build and pretty good looking. I've seen all these kids before in the diner and in school but Slim and Justin were in the grade below me so I don't really know any of them. My friend, Molly, dated Slim for a semester or less.

"Ben should be with them," Natalie says. "I wonder if he's trying to call me and thinks I'm mad at him or that my mom is making me stay at home." I can feel her anxiety and try to override it by taking a few deep calming breaths.

I hold the water bottle I had been carrying up to my mouth and pretend to take a drink. "Let's go over and talk to Justin, because I know him better, and see if he knows anything."

As I start to head over to Justin, Ben walks up and joins his friends. He runs his fingers through his shaggy black hair and gives one of his friends a low five. His mood seems pretty chill. I'm sure he's wondering where his girlfriend is, though. I decide to go over to them still, ask them how they are and start talking, maybe casually bringing up Natalie's name.

"Victoria," I hear a familiar voice from behind me yelling my name. Justin and Ben both look over and see me staring at them. I turn quickly to respond to Piper but she pulls my arm and shoves me into the side of a nearby vendor. "I've been looking for you everywhere. Why didn't you call me back?" She seems rather angry with me. *I have no idea she could get this upset about a dang missed call.*

"My phone is in the car," I say, looking past her and trying not to lose Ben. As I'm looking at him, I see Andrea walk up to him and start talking. I see him shake his head at her and she looks worried.

"What the heck are they talking about?" Natalie asks. *I can imagine her squinting her eyes to focus on their lips.*

"Dude, I have something really important to tell you. We saw Ryan." I accidentally lock eyes with Ben, and we stare at each other. Piper notices my distracted face and turns to look at what I'm staring at. "Do you know him?"

"Who?" I turn my gaze to her.

"That guy that was staring at you."

"No, I didn't see him looking at me." I steal another glance as Piper turns to look at Ben again, probably making sure she's not crazy. Andrea gently touches Ben's arm, leans in to whisper something in his ear and walks off. Oh, no. My nerves seem a little frayed. "Don't be jealous…" I start to tell Natalie to keep her calm, but of course, Piper hears me.

"Jealous? Girlfriend, I got a man," she says jokingly to me.

"I know. I was kidding."

"Did you hear what I said?" She doesn't pause for my response. "I said we saw Ryan. I have to tell you something." Once again we are interrupted, this time by Grant walking up with a huge malicious smile on his face. He comes up from behind her and kisses her neck. She gasps and whirls around, about to punch her attacker when she realizes it's Grant. I smile at their encounter and switch my eyes back to Ben. *Oh, crap, he's gone. Crap.*

"V, where'd he go?" Natalie shouts.

"Hey, V. What's up?" Grant says, smiling at me, while holding Piper. His smile is distracting; it's once again malicious or secretive or something. *There is so much going on and I can't talk to Natalie in the presence of human beings. I need to be alone. Well, alone with Natalie.*

"'Sup, Grant? Hey, guys, I'll meet up with you later. I have to…" and before I can finish my sentence, Ryan walks up to join Grant. My jaw drops and my mind goes blank.

Chapter 6

I Seriously Didn't See That Coming

My mind starts back up and I can't stop staring at him. He looks beyond gorgeous.

"Oh, hey, V. Piper said you'd be here tonight. How are you?" He is wearing slightly fitted jeans that sag a smidge at his waist and a white polo shirt; his aviator sunglasses sitting on top of his shaggy reddish-brown hair. His usually pale Irish skin is no more. Here in front of me stands a tanned and toned MacKenna. He smells divine.

"Wow. With all this internal angst, you've got to be sweating, V," Natalie teases. "Boob sweat?" she giggles.

I literally shake my head, maybe once again trying to shake her out of my mind.

"Hi, Ryan." I'm barely able make out his name because all of a sudden I seem parched.

I hear Grant stifle a laugh and Ryan looks in his direction. *Ryan has no idea the effect he has on me.*

"Ryan just got back from vacation Thursday night," Piper says, for Ryan's sake I'm sure, as if this is news to me. "I'm sure he'll tell you all about it but I have to use the ladies room. Come with me."

I take my eyes off Ryan finally to look at Piper. I'm not sure if, in our long-standing friendship, she's ever invited me to the bathroom with her. I know that's a girl thing to do but, honestly, I don't think it's ever happened.

As she grabs my hand to whisk me off to the gossip stalls, a friendly young man walks up and hands Ryan a snow cone and kisses him on the cheek.

"Thanks. I just love piña colada," Ryan smiles, sweetly at him.

I make a strange noise. I'm ashamed to say it is loud. It may be a mash-up between a grunt as if I am hit in the stomach, a gasp as if a lightbulb has gone off and a guffaw, as if to say 'I am the stupidest person in the world'.

The new guy, Grant, and Ryan all stare at me bewildered, as Piper squeezes my hand and pulls me hard toward the bathroom. I'm glad for the hand, even if she is squeezing it too tight, because I am so dizzy.

When we finally get in there, all my emotions that have been cinched and ignored come flying out.

"What in the hell is that?" I scream at her, as if it's her fault.

"I tried telling you ten times, Victoria," she yells back, equally loud and exaggerating.

"Next time tell me to shut up and blurt it out." I kick the wall. *I'll feel sorry for that later.*

"I'm sorry, V. I called you a bunch of times. I tried to tell you before he met up with us. I had already invited him to join us before he introduced me to Evan."

I pace up and down the bathroom, fuming. "I am such an idiot. We were gonna have babies, Pipe." With so many emotions running through me the past twenty-four hours, the tears just run down my face. Even though Ryan didn't know I liked him, for a long time at that, I still feel humiliated. All of my daydreams and fantasies are worthless now. My two pale Irish sons and one olive-toned Italian daughter have vanished. I feel hollow. I feel stupid. Naïve.

She walks over and gives me a side-by-side hug and tilts her head to mine. "I know, V. I'm sorry."

"No, I'm sorry. I don't know why I'm crying." I wipe my face and grab a paper towel to dab my eyes. So much for my perfect makeup. I sigh in the mirror.

"You still look great, V." Piper encourages me. "Ryan told Grant that all through high school he dated girls to see if his feelings for guys would go away but they didn't. When he went on vacation, he met Evan who happens to live like forty-five minutes from here. He came home early to tell his parents who took it rather well, if you care to know," she says very gently, almost whispering to me.

I nod, as I am speechless. I blow my nose and take a few deep breaths.

"Pipe, I gotta go, OK? I'm sorry. I gotta go."

"I'll tell them you have a headache. Call me later, though, OK?"

"Sure." I walk out, not knowing what I'm doing or where I'm going.

"V, I'm sorry," Natalie whispers, feeling I'm still pretty upset.

"It's fine," I lie. "Don't worry about it." I pocket my heartbreak until later when I'm at home and can cry into my pillow. I take a deep breath. "Let's find Ben," I say.

I walk aimlessly around, not finding Ben or any of his friends. I realize for the past few minutes I've been walking way out of range of the bonfire's light and warmth.

I see a tiny fire with a lone familiar face and two giggling girls retreating.

"He is so weird," one of the girls giggles.

"This town doesn't need another Kooky."

I take that as my cue to go speak to this guy and see if he knows anything. Finally, I don't have to pretend to take a sip from my water so I can speak to Natalie without looking crazy. No one else is this far out from the bonfire.

"Hey, I think that guy knows Kook," I rephrase myself not wanting to offend her, "John. I'm going to go talk to him and see if he knows anything."

"Do you know him?"

"Not really, but he graduated with my sister a few years ago so that may help. I've seen him in the diner with John. Maybe he knows something."

"OK. Good luck, Joe."

"OK, who the heck is Joe?"

"Good grief, V. Joe Hardy from The Hardy Boys. You need to do some reading."

"Sorry, but my grandparents didn't read me to sleep."

It's always a little creepy to see someone who is about three to five years older than everyone else at the party. Makes one wonder what went wrong. Then again, there's not much else to do in this town and what's wrong with hanging out on a Saturday night? I shake my head, trying to rid it of this ridiculous dead-end argument.

OK, let's see if Kooky told this guy anything about murdering Natalie.

"It's so warm over here," I smile gently at him.

He looks up and takes a drink.

"Why do you look familiar?" he asks, with a quizzical look. This usually happens when people have known my sister but haven't seen her in a while then they see me. We can't help but look very much alike.

"You probably know my sister, Valentina." Deep down I'm hoping they weren't mortal enemies because then my plan will be washed out. He smiles at her name, releasing me from my internal struggle.

"Valentina," he muses at her name. "Yeah, we graduated together. How is she?"

"She's good. She's at Brown University now. I'm sure you knew she went to Idaho Community for two years."

"Yeah. I was in the engineering program."

"Oh, really," I feign interest. "You have to be pretty intelligent and good with your hands then." I try to amp up the charm by smiling and twirling my hair. If he's interested in me, I can direct this conversation where I want it to go and get some information on Kooky. He smiles too warmly at me and says, "Yes. I am both. Valentina's sister, I didn't catch your name."

"Victoria. And you are?"

"Alan."

I take a seat across from him on the ground.

"You work at the diner, right?" I wasn't aware he has seen me there, although it's not exactly surprising, either.

"Yeah. Almost a year now." To take control of the conversation and make sure it heads in the direction I want it to go, I say, "You should have been at the diner the other day when Kooky was going off about some nonsense. He was off the wall."

"Oh, man," he sighs in agreement. "Yeah, that guy has a few screws loose."

"Yeah, he scares me. My boss, Mike, kicked him out before things got too out of control."

He looks down at his cup and squirms uncomfortably. He actually turns from his natural skin tone to white and then green.

"Are you OK?" I worry he's about to be sick all over the place.

He lets out a tiny burp and then swallows, scrunching his face in the process.

"Yeah, I'm all right. That guy Kooky freaks me out." He's whispering now and I'm taken back to my childhood when my brother would tell ghost stories around the campfire, trying to torture my sister and me, which he always succeeded in doing.

"We went hunting a few weeks back..." He pauses, shaking his head a bit, perhaps to rid it of a horrible memory. "He did something awful. I can't get it out of my head."

My nerves are starting to get the better of me. I'm intrigued to know what happened but, at the same time, if it ruined this guy, what makes me think I can handle it?

"What did he do?" I persist, wanting, no, needing to know more.

"We went out by the mountain to hunt some wild boar. He took a shot and missed. Well, he was real pissed. I tried telling him to blow it off; it happens, ya know? It wasn't a big deal. Anyway, we kept on the trail of the boar and the whole time he was complaining about missing the shot and cussing up a storm. Eventually, we caught up to it and I was ready to take my shot but he said he wanted to take it. I let him, of course, because he was so pissed about missing earlier. So he took the shot but he didn't aim for the kill and he had the right shot. He only injured it. I got set up to shoot so I could do it right, ya know, humanely; but he told me he had this, so he walked up to it and I thought he was going to take another shot but he didn't." He pauses briefly and looks sick again. I worry that this isn't going to be good and I don't want to hear anymore. I start to say that I've heard enough, but he keeps going.

"I don't want to hear this," Natalie says, drowning him out.

"Me either. Sing," I whisper, trying hard not to move my mouth. It takes Natalie only a second to understand why. She starts to sing loudly.

I continue looking at Alan, giving him looks of disgust at points that I think could be the right places in the one-sided conversation I can't hear. This poor guy looks disturbed. I bet he doesn't eat meat anymore.

I mentally run through everything I know to make sure I have it all straight. Remembering Kooky came into the diner what must've been Wednesday and yelled about some lady wanting to ruin his son's life, Kandi just found out Ben and Natalie were dating so she got mad. Kooky was pissed at Natalie's mom, Kandi. She wanted to call the cops on Ben and there was no way Kooky was going to allow that to happen. *So did he kill Natalie to save his son?* I'm starting to think so.

Relentlessly, Alan has finished talking and Natalie ends her church lullaby. At least he was able to get that off his chest to someone.

"That's awful," I say quietly.

"Yeah, it was. I should have known. I've seen his shed of hanging dead animals. I should have known," he repeats. "I'm not hanging around him anymore. You make sure you stay away from that guy. He's not just Kooky; he's a flippin' psycho."

Another cue? More confirmation.

"Thanks. I will." I jump up and brush my bum off. "I have to get going."

"Where is it you have to go?" He returns with that warm smile, his apparent distress now forgotten.

"Bed," I blurt out quickly and he smiles even bigger.

"Not what she meant, you scoundrel," Natalie says protectively. *I imagine her giving him a wicked evil eye.*

"I have to work in the morning," I add and practically run off before he can say anything else.

"That guy is creepy."

"Why? Because he liked me?" I say a little offended.

"Uh, no, sunshine, because he just told you a horror story and without delay was ready to…"

I cut her off, knowing where she is going with that. "All right, I get it. Is that verification enough for you?" I ask in regards to that horror story we didn't get to hear.

"Um, yeah. We have to go to Kooky's house." This is the first time I hear her say his nickname. I guess she really is convinced.

"Wait, why do we need to go there?"

"To snoop around for evidence. You heard Alan say Kooky has a shed of dead animals. Maybe that's where he's keeping my clothes and purse and stuff."

I grunt and get into my car. I drive off quickly, turning up the music to drown out my worries.

I park a block away. With stealth-like moves, I trespass onto Kooky's property, which isn't too hard. I pretty much walk onto the side yard and creep up to the shed. *We'll be looking for evidence that John killed Natalie. A gun or a bloody hammer, as Natalie so eloquently put it once. Maybe he even took her clothes and piled them in a corner. Anything will be helpful at this point.*

"Wow, Ben's already home," Natalie says when we spot his truck parked next to the house.

"Guess he didn't find what he was looking for."

I have a small LED light on my key chain and a mini flashlight in my back pocket. I click the button and a sharp blue light shines out. I head toward the shed door, ninja-style, of course, with my eyes shooting from left to right and for some reason even up to the roof. *Yeah, V, like someone is going to be up there waiting for you; they'd fall right through.*

109

The shed is old and leaning heavily to the left. The gray paint is chipped, and the roof is caved in. It looks to be an abandoned building, one that should be left alone but, as in some horror movie, I head straight for the door.

Chapter 7

The Things I Do For You

It's terrifying.

"V? Are you OK? It's getting tense in here." She makes it sound as if she's hiding in a small closet, talking to me on a walkie-talkie.

"I don't want to go in there, Natalie." My voice is shaky, and I can't seem to move my feet.

"V..." I imagine her putting her hands on my shoulders and looking sternly into my eyes as she stands over me, "You can do this. Don't be afraid. Maybe this is the one thing you're destined to do...solve a small town murder and go on to become a detective. Nancy, you can do this."

She actually has me going until she adds the Nancy part. I roll my eyes, take a deep breath and notice it's absolutely silent outside. No owls, no barking dogs or passing cars. Silence.

With trembling fingers, I creak open the shed door. It's weathered and rusty but I manage to slip in without making further noise. My heart is racing. It feels as if it's going to pound right out of my chest. The smell is awful, so I wrap my shawl around my nose and mouth. I squeeze my eyes shut out of fear.

"Get the flashlight and try to stay calm," Natalie coaxes.

I get out the mini flashlight and my eyes widen at the sight.

"Kooky, indeed," Natalie whispers.

I am motionless as I take in all of the dead carcasses hanging from the metal rack to my right. I'm quite sure he doesn't intend to eat rancid meat, so why are they hanging from hooks? I don't want to know. My stomach muscles contract. I gag, dry heave and spit on the floor. My knees buckle when I try to stand upright again. I can feel my face and hands getting clammy. Bloody utensils are everywhere. Everything is dirty, bloody or rusty and I want to vomit. I guess that would be from the stench. I hear a vibrating noise but, before I can question it, a squealing noise on my left scares me to death and I drop the flashlight.

"What is that?" Natalie asks, nervously.

"I don't know. It was something in a cage on that table." I reach down to grab the flashlight and shine it on the cage. My hands are shaking so badly I have to use two hands to hold the mini flashlight steady. "It's a squirrel, no doubt on its way to meet its maker."

112

"You have to set it free, V."

"I know. I just don't want it to bite me."

I see a metal rod nearby. I grab a work glove and without putting the disgusting thing on, I use it as a pot holder to grab the metal rod. I try to steady my hand so I can open the latch with the rod. It doesn't work so I toss the rod back on the table, making a thumping sound and flip the latch quickly. It stays closed but not locked, so I tug on the door a bit and stand back again, quickly. The squirrel races out of the cage and scurries around the floor until it finds the rusty door I came through and escapes. I breathe deeply into my shawl. I have to get on with this and get out of here before anyone comes out here and before the smell makes me vomit all over the floor.

I search the table frantically, finding nothing. I throw the pot holder work glove on the stupid table.

"Natalie, I don't see anything. I mean, all of this stuff has dried blood on it from these animals. Maybe I can call the sheriff and have him come take a look out here. By that time, everyone will probably realize you're missing and they'll take him in for questioning because he's a psycho."

Before Natalie answers me, the flashlight shines on something on the corner of the desk.

"What is that?" I ask as I squint, trying to focus on the object.

"I can't tell. Get closer." The object vibrates, and as with everything in this shed, it scares me.

"Geez, I'm getting so sick of this damn shed."

"Me, too, V."

I walk over to the shiny object and see that it's a phone. It has a purple and white glittering case, not one I would picture Kooky picking out for himself in a store. I reach to grab the phone.

"Don't touch it, V," Natalie shouts.

I cower in fear. "What the hell, Natalie. You can feel my nerves. I'm already frightened," I say through gritting teeth. "Don't do that." I swat my hand in the air as if to smack her, refusing to actually hit myself. I've already done that before.

"I'm sorry. I was thinking fingerprints. You don't want your fingerprints on anything. I'm pretty sure that's my phone." I grab the nasty rag next to the phone and try hard not to think about why it's crusty as I turn over the phone. Still using the rag, I press the circle button to awaken the screen. A photo of Ben and Natalie are on the wallpaper. I stare at it for a moment. This is the first image I have ever seen of Natalie. It's only her profile since she is looking and laughing at Ben. It's such a carefree scene: a young girl laughing, probably with not a care in the world in that moment, just having a good time. The screen goes black.

"Yep," she whispers.

I wish I could insert a sarcastic remark as she always does but I am panicking. I don't know if it's her emotions or my own at this point but I don't care; I can feel someone is about to be hysterical.

"Natalie, that's it. I can't do this anymore. I'm scared, and this freaking guy is crazy. He has to have killed you. There's no one else. I'm going to the sheriff." Tears start streaming down my face. The adrenaline is slowly leveling out and I can feel I'm about to lose it. *I'm no Nancy Drew. I'm no detective. I'm an eighteen-year-old girl who works at a diner and who rather liked having a normal life. This is too much on my own. I have to get out of here.*

"OK, I believe you. But we have to keep our head about this." *Funny way to put it.* "You can't go to the sheriff's office as upset as you are. Let's get out of here and go home. We can call in a tip tomorrow or something."

"OK," I cry in a whisper. I try to move as quickly and yet as quietly as I can to get through the creaky door and run to my car. *I hate thinking someone could be behind me.* I get into my car safely and feel much better with a seat at my back. I lock the doors and, because of having watched too many movies and television shows, I turn to look in the backseat. Empty. Good.

"Natalie, I'm so sorry. I mean, obviously we already know you're dead and someone killed you. I'm sorry this has happened at all. Are you OK?"

She hesitates to answer, but finally replies, "Yeah. I'm sad for Ben. I mean his father is a rumored murderer, so the town can have something to gossip about but now he really is a murderer. I wish my mom hadn't interfered. Maybe she ticked Kooky off and he thought my mom was going to cause trouble for Ben and he needed to take things into his own filthy hands. I wish I could see Ben, be there for him, especially if he's going to lose both of his parents."

I can't say anything to make her feel better so I stay silent. Sometimes there's nothing to say and silence is the best response.

It's a quiet drive home. I let the day's events weave through my mind as a vine, some of it smooth and some with piercing thorns. *Saturday morning pancakes, smooth; seeing Kandi at the diner, thorn; getting to know Natalie at the hot spring and cave, smooth; finding Natalie's earring, hmm, smooth and a thorn; learning Ryan's preference in humans, big thorn with poison; discovering Natalie's cell phone in Kooky's shed, another big thorn. I know it's helpful uncovering all these clues and finding out information but it still stings, especially for Natalie because her feelings can override my own.* We pull up to my house and it finally sinks in, I'm exhausted.

My parents are already in bed but they left the porch light on for me. I chug a glass of orange juice and lethargically ascend the stairs for a shower. The bonfire has left me hovering in a smelly ball of smoke and mesquite. As I'm washing my hair Natalie finally speaks.

"What are you going to do tomorrow about my phone?" she asks, softly.

"Well, I was thinking of going to the sheriff's office and reporting I heard some things at the bonfire that concern me, having to do with you not being seen since Thursday and putting John "Kooky" Harper's name in the mix. Maybe they will go ahead and start their investigation. Who knows? That's the best I can come up with."

Natalie doesn't respond, which is unusual. "What are your thoughts?"

"Yeah, that's good."

"What's wrong?"

"Just feeling as tired as you are, I guess."

"OK, I'm going to bed in a minute and we'll both feel better in the morning. Keep your chin up."

"Only if you point it up."

I smile. There's my girl.

I finish up in the bathroom and hop into bed.

"Good night, Natalie. I hope everything turns out swell."

"Now you sound like a Hardy Boy," she says and I smile. "Good night, V."

And with that, I drift off to a night filled with colorful dreams.

I'm running as fast as I can through the woods. The brown tree trunks are illuminated from within. The leaves are a fluorescent green. Purple flowers are glowing like night-lights and little flying bugs are shining a bright yellow and orange. I'm screaming but no one can hear me. Vines are reaching out for me, trying to wrap around my arms and legs. I'm being ripped open by huge thorns piercing my arms and my cheek but I keep running. I trip on something and fall flat on my face. He's going to catch me if I don't get up. I look back as I'm getting up and realize I tripped over a body; a young girl with beautiful red hair lies there, dead. Her pale skin turns into a charred black corpse with flecks blowing off her into the wind until she completely disappears. I hear him running after me. I get to my feet and run as fast as I can. I can hear him calling my name, "Victoria. Stop running. You're only making it worse. Victoria."

I hate how he snarls my name. I keep screaming and crying, my throat sore and cracking. All the colors darken and everything is black. I fall into the hot spring but come up for air and decide to take a deep breath and go under and wait until he runs past me. My heart is racing and my body is shaking but I stay under the warm water to save my life. After a minute, I need to come up for air. I open my eyes under the water but it's still pitch black. Out of nowhere a bright light shines from the sky and there his ugly, hateful, dirty and murderous face screams my name from above as he pulls me out of the water.

I wake up, gasping for air and grabbing my throat. I sit up, panting and shaking and trying to catch my breath.

"Victoria." A familiar, yet worried voice calls to me. "Are you OK? I couldn't wake you. What's going on?" Natalie asks, with immediate concern.

I throw myself back on my pillow and close my eyes but I open them quickly in fear I might see his face again.

"V?"

"It was just a dream. I mean a nightmare, a freaking horrible nightmare." I lie there, taking deep breaths to regulate my heart rate.

"I didn't know what was happening but your emotions were horrifying. I was so scared but I had no idea why. I kept calling your name, trying to wake you up."

"Did you happen to tell me I was making it worse?"

"No? Why?"

"I was being chased and that's what he said to me. That by running, I was making it worse."

"Oh, gosh, V. That's awful. I'm sorry. Are you all right? You still seem a little shaken. Who was it?"

"It was Kooky but he transformed into that guy, Alan, from the bonfire then back to Kooky."

I lie in bed for a few more minutes, calming myself by looking at my cherry blossom mural.

I go to wash my face, relieving the clammy feeling and I descend downstairs for a small breakfast. My stomach isn't keen on eating much, considering last night's events at the shed. Plus, that I need to go to the sheriff's office, which makes me extremely nervous. I can't seem to eat when I'm extremely nervous. I grab my teacup and a nice, light, lemony tea bag. As I'm filling the kettle, my mom shuffles in wearing her slippers and tying her silky robe.

"Hey."

"Morning, V. Oh, my goodness, did you hear the news about that girl?" she speaks quietly, as if there are eavesdroppers nearby.

It's such a broad question. I have no idea if she's talking about Natalie or someone else. "No. What girl?"

She grabs a packet of muffin mix and fills me in. "Oh, there's a missing girl from here. A young girl. They think she may be a runaway but they aren't sure. They're going to have a search for her this afternoon over in the woods."

My heart skips a beat.

"Dude, she's talking about me."

"What's her name? Anyone I know?"

"Oh, probably not. She's younger, like fourteen or so. I can't remember her name, though. She's a real cutie. I hope nothing bad happened to her."

She whips the batter and fills the muffin pan.

119

"V, you have to turn on the news. My mom probably figured out I wasn't at Andrea's."

The kettle whistles and I hesitate. I choose the TV over the whistling.

"Do you want me to get that?" Mom asks, referring to the boiling water.

"Yeah," I almost whisper. I walk to the living room and turn on the TV.

Yep. There's a beautiful picture of Natalie taking up most of the screen. I turn up the volume. The reporter is talking about other news stories but the newscast is splitting the screen with pictures of Natalie. The word **MISSING** is in big bold letters at the top of her picture, and her name appears below it. Dad walks in and stands next to me.

"Morning, Victoria."

"Hey, Dad," I answer but keep my eyes on the screen, waiting for the reporter to return to the story.

"Isn't that awful? I hope nothing happened to the little girl."

The reporter starts the story. I listen intently so I won't miss a thing.

Apparently Kandi went to Andrea's house Saturday afternoon and found neither of them was there. I may have given her the idea to do that. Andrea's mom said Natalie hadn't been there in days. Kandi then went to Ben's house, demanding he let her in but he refused. After no luck in finding Natalie at the bonfire, Kandi went to the police station. The investigation is only beginning. Andrea is the only person questioned as of yet. The police have no further information. Mom hands me my tea and sits on the couch. I join her.

"Thank you."

"Do you know her?" she asks. Mom is looking me over in concern. I must look pretty shaken.

"No, but I'm pretty sure her mom came into the diner, worrying about her. She told me she hadn't seen her daughter since Thursday. They had an argument. That was yesterday morning when she came in."

"Oh. It must be the same girl. That's awful."

The phone rings and my dad answers it. He speaks for a few minutes and hangs up.

"That was Esther from church. She said no service this morning but we'll have a vigil for that missing girl."

"Natalie," I interrupt.

"Natalie," he repeats. "The ladies are taking names to help in searching the woods this afternoon. I told her we would go."

"Absolutely," Mom agrees. "V, you want to go?"

"Sure." I sip my tea, knowing they probably won't find any evidence. The thought sparks a question. "Which area are they searching?"

"Kent. That's the one near her friend's house, where she was last known to be," Dad replies.

Well, I have no idea if there is other evidence but I certainly have her earring. I wonder if I should turn it in to the police. I mean, there's no reason why I have to be the one to solve this murder. I can hand it over to the police and let them figure it out. Mom startles me out of my thoughts.

"V, would Piper want to do the search?"

"I'm sure she'd want to help but she's covering for me pretty much this entire week, starting today."

"Oh, OK. Well, I'll call her parents to see if they can help."

I get up, finishing my tea in the kitchen and picking at a muffin.

"Do you think Ben heard the news?"

"Oh, definitely."

"I hope Andrea gives as much information as she can. I hate that she had to be questioned, in that she was the last one to see me. Gosh, I bet all my friends from school are freakin' out."

"Of course, they are. Your mom is probably a frantic mess, too," I whisper.

"I wonder if they'll find something we missed yesterday?"

That reminds me about the earring. I go upstairs so we can plan this out. I go back to the pants I wore yesterday and take the earring out of the pocket. I put it on my desk.

"Should I still go to the sheriff? To tell them about Kooky's shed and give them your earring?"

"Oh," she whines, "I wanted you to keep the earring. You can call in an anonymous tip about Kooky."

"All right." I lie on my bed and check my phone. "Do I need to read these aloud or can you read them because my eyes are looking at the words?"

"I can read them 'cause you're looking at them long enough."

"Oh, cool." I respond to about fifteen text messages regarding Natalie and the search. A few texts ask if I heard Ryan was gay and one from Piper who asks if I heard Kooky was being brought in for questioning. *That text is from about five minutes ago. They must be playing the news at the diner.*

"Well, the sheriff must have their own suspicions," Natalie remarks.

"Guess so. We keep lucking out, in a way."

"What do you mean?"

"I was all nervous about questioning people at the bonfire but it turned out I didn't really have to do it. We found Alan and he gave us plenty of information. We decided to go to the police station but you were already reported as missing and now I was going to give an anonymous tip about Kooky but he's already been in for questioning. Our work seems a few steps behind the official investigation."

"Yeah, but at least we seem to be on the right track. Even if the police solve it first, it's not a big deal. The point is, it gets solved."

"True, true. Should I go into town to the diner and ask Piper what else she knows? Maybe after that we can go over and join the team searching the woods."

"Sounds good to me. Let me call my mom first," Natalie teases.

"Ha, Ha." I turn on my IPod and get dressed, making sure to put jeans and my hiking boots on for the search of the woods. I grab the earring off the desk and put it in my pocket. I feel as if it will bring us luck today. I put my makeup on in the bathroom. Now that Vincent and Valentina are gone, I get the bathroom all to myself. I have more room to keep my makeup, hair products and lotions all over the counters.

"Hey, how are you doing about Ryan?" She sounds nervous asking but not enough to make me feel nervous, too.

"I haven't thought about it, actually. Thanks for bringing it up." I smile in the mirror.

"You're so pretty, V. I'm sure there will be hundreds of guys at college who will be putty in your hands; add in you're sporty and smart, God help you."

I blush and feel giddy inside. "OK. Thank you. Nobody talks to me that way. You're making me uncomfortable but thank you. I kind of find the whole Ryan thing silly."

"Why?"

"Because I invested so much energy on a fantasy, a dream. It sucks because I get that way about guys. I get silly."

"Yeah, but just think when it really happens you won't feel silly. You will have, as you said, invested all these hopes and dreams and it won't all be for nothing."

"I guess we'll see."

"Well, hopefully, I'll see it from a different perspective. You can't have me there ruining it with sarcastic comments."

"Now that is absolutely true." We laugh and I finish getting ready.

I go downstairs to ask what time the search begins. My parents are both getting ready for church. Mom looks at my casual attire.

"Aren't you going to church for the vigil?"

"No, I'm going to the diner to talk to Piper for a bit. I'll meet you at Kent for the search. When is it?"

"I'm not sure yet. I have to ask the ladies at church. I can text you later."

"Sure. Are Piper's parents going, too?"

"Amanda and Bruce? Yep, they are on board."

"OK. See you later. Bye, Dad," I yell so he can hear me from the bathroom. He opens the door with a toothbrush in his mouth. Amid toothpaste foam and all, he says, "No church?"

"No. I have business to attend to."

"Aw. OK. Give me a kiss... " He has purposely let toothpaste dribble down his chin.

I scream, "No, gross." Then I rush out the door. I can hear them laughing behind me.

"Your dad is funny."

"Yeah. A nerd, too." I grab my purse and keys and go to my car. It's a nice, quiet drive to the diner. Natalie and I listen to music and get lost in our own separate thoughts. Although I think the drive is quiet, somehow when we enter downtown, it gets even quieter. Bunches of green ribbons are on every post. Pictures of Natalie are on every window of every store. How startling it is and yet so touching that overnight the town has changed, people have come together to help Kandi and the sheriff find Natalie.

"Wow, I don't even have one thing to say," Natalie declares.

"Me either." I've never seen anything like it but that's a good thing. I pull up to the diner and get out. I catch myself staring at the poster of Natalie's perfect smiling face at the lake. "You're missed, girl. That's for sure."

Piper makes my heart skip when she bangs on the window, waving me in. Not sure the people she reached across at the booth appreciate it very much.

Piper, of course, doesn't notice. I barely step in before Piper grabs me and shoves me into an empty booth. She's been somewhat hostile toward me lately.

"Are you OK?"

She has no idea I'm possessed by Natalie's spirit, so her open-ended question confuses me.

"Yeah. Why?"

"I told Ryan last night you weren't feeling good. They all seemed to buy it. You didn't call me last night but this morning you replied about psycho Kooky being questioned. So, you're avoiding talking to me about Ryan and you shouldn't. You need to get it out and vent before you burst."

"I did vent. Remember the bathroom? My toe is sore from kicking the trashcan. I'm fine. Really." I look her straight in the eyes. I can't even tell if I'm lying or not but all the better, to change subjects.

"Are you sure? 'Cause I know how much you liked him."

"Yes, I promise." Still not sure if I'm lying. "Now what the hell is going on with this missing girl?"

Piper doesn't miss any details as she spills everything she's heard and knows, which isn't more than I already know. Kooky was brought in for questioning because, apparently, someone called in a tip regarding his outburst in the diner the other day. The caller heard through the grapevine Ben was dating Natalie and so assumed his rant was about Kandi and Natalie. Mike, our boss, gives her several grunts every now and then to let her know she needs to work. After a few minutes, he turns up the volume in his nonchalant clearing of his throat. She rolls her eyes and gets up to fill some patrons' mugs of coffee.

Piper comes back with a mug of tea and the Grizzly Bear platter. "Eat up. You'll need it for the search later."

"Your parents are going. Are you going?"

"No. Mike says we have to stay open for the after church crowd and anyone else who wanders in."

"OK. I figured as much. Thanks for the breakfast."

She gives me a wink and goes back to tend to her tables. I slowly eat my stack of French toast and bacon, waiting for my mom to text me. I'm certainly going to miss working here and interacting with all the people. On the other hand, I'm very excited to go to college and not have to worry about working.

Church must be over because my mom finally texts me the search is on for noon. That's about forty-five minutes from now. I decide to try to convince Mike to make sandwiches, on the house, of course, for the volunteers in the search. He compromises by sending someone to the store to buy loaves of cheap sandwich bread, instead of using the nicer baguettes he has here. I don't argue. He does have a business to run. I text Mom so she can spread the word about the free sandwiches for volunteers and they have to come to the back entrance of the diner to take one.

I say bye to Piper and Ava and make my way over to Kent woods.

Chapter 8

Right Place at the Right Time, Or No?

I'm glad we're looking in Kent woods and not Burton State Park. Burton State Park has mountain lions, hills and steep slopes. At least here it's relatively flat and the trees are spread out, not allowing too many predators to remain unseen. The search team should have protection, just in case, blow horns, bear spray and, of course, the rangers and officers will be there looking out for us. I don't think we'll go too deep into the woods but who knows? I park on the side of the road as does everyone else. I put my hair in a ponytail and put on a BSU hat.

"Man, it's hot," I say to myself, forgetting someone in my body is actually there to hear me.

There are several people already here but it's still not noon yet. I see Mrs. Diaz who heads up the local chapter of the Girl Scouts. She is in full authority mode, directing people where to go. I see Camden and decide to go say "hi" first, before reporting for duty.

"This is like a terrible Easter egg hunt."

I giggle at her analogy. I guess she's right.

"Hey, Camden, how's it going?"

"Pretty good. We have all the groups set up; we just need all the volunteers to show so we can start."

"Oh, great. I'm glad to see so many people coming together and helping out."

"Yeah." Camden checks her phone. *She must have gotten an update from the news or someone texted her because she has new information to share.*

"Hey, someone from a nearby town, Nampa, I think, is missing, too. A young girl possibly related to Natalie's disappearance."

"So maybe they're looking for a serial killer?" I think aloud.

"Oh, don't say that, V. Be optimistic. We're searching for evidence that someone kidnapped her, or maybe she ran away or went hiking and got lost. We're going to find her today."

I am taken aback, realizing almost everyone here probably thinks these same things. They are searching with optimism and hope. Who am I to take that away from them? I smile at Camden. With my throat a little choked up, I reply, "You're absolutely right."

She nods and puts her summer hat on. "It's getting so hot. I hope we start soon."

Mrs. Diaz comes over to us and fills me in on how the search will go and what area each group is covering. She directs me to go tell the cheerleading squad the same thing. I walk over to the squad and get a weird feeling in my stomach. Not quite sure what that feeling is, I mumble to Natalie before I reach the squad, "Are these all of your old friends?"

"Yeah, most of them. The younger ones are freshmen, so I know all of them. The captains are older, so I don't know them as well. The one with brown hair and the white tank top is Evelyn. We were pretty much best friends since elementary school.

"She got jealous when I started to hang out with Andrea so much. She was pretty angry that I dropped cheerleading. She didn't talk to me after that."

"Geez. Sorry."

"No, I understand. Change is hard to accept and I hurt her feelings. I wasn't being a good friend but that one right there," I imagine she points but wait for her to finish before asking who, "the one in the purple halter thing is vicious. That's Jena."

I bend down and pretend to tie my boots since I've arrived at their group and don't want anyone to see me talking.

"How could she not like you?"

"I have no idea. It almost seemed as if it offended her personally when I quit cheerleading. She always said rude crap to me when I walked by in the hall at school. We also had a class together last semester and anything

131

I said she had a freakin' rude remark for it. Like one time I slipped up and said something about King Caesar and she laughed ridiculously loud and said 'It's not King Caesar, you idiot; it's just Caesar.' She always tried to make me feel stupid."

The queen herself interrupts us. "So are you going to tell us what we're supposed to be doing, or what? We already had to cancel cheerleading practice; I don't want to be out here all day."

I stand up, happy to realize I'm at least three inches taller than she is, thanks to my boots. I'm eager to put this broad in her place but I don't want to stoop to her level by calling her a selfish brat or something worse.

So I kindly respond, "Yes, Mrs. Diaz wants everyone in this group to stand side by side in a straight line a few feet apart. When you walk, walk slowly and look closely at the ground for any items such as a cell phone, purse, female clothing, etc. If you find anything, you have to yell out to your group leader and your line will stop. The authorities will come over to collect the evidence."

The girls stare at me. I know they understand; I just assumed I would hear an 'OK' or something. So I have to ask, "OK? Any questions?"

Still no one answers but they shake their heads 'no'.

"I'm group leader. If you find something, tell me first." Jena ordered.

She is certainly getting on my nerves. I take a deep breath and finish up so I can flee her presence. "Thanks for coming out today to help with the search. Let's all keep positive thoughts and, of course, always keep hope alive." I feel like such a hypocrite saying that, as I stand here, knowing the truth.

Jena scoffs and loudly whispers to the person standing next to her. "This is so ridiculous. Natalie got mad at Ben because he was going to break up with her because her mom is a flippin' psycho so she ran away because she just wants attention." They both snicker at her comment. I glance at Evelyn who looks as if she's about to defend Natalie but she hesitates and keeps her lips sealed. My blood is boiling and I can't seem to control my own feelings. Natalie says a few choice words about Jena but I try to block them out and defend Natalie in my own words.

Speaking a smidge too loudly so as to muffle Natalie's rant, I start without a pause, "I hope there isn't any jealousy toward a loving mother who worries about her young daughter dating an older guy. You should prepare yourself for many breakups in the future because I'm certain anyone who encounters you for longer than forty-five seconds will inevitably try to escape your loathsome presence. Sorry the disappearance of a beautiful, intelligent and, I've heard, very funny young woman has put such an inconvenience in your life. What a shame to be so devoured with oneself."

As I turn to walk away, I notice several girls trying to hide their smiles. That is probably something they have all wanted to say for a long time.

"Let that sink in," I say to Natalie.

"I can't believe you said that. Loathsome? Wow,"

"Well, it was uncharacteristic of me, for sure. I've never done that before but she ticked me off. I felt provoked."

"Well...that could have been my fault. I couldn't calm myself down so I totally overrode your emotions."

"Hey, at least I didn't repeat what you were saying."

We both laugh and I realize I have to stop talking before someone notices. I rejoin Camden because we're in the same group.

"Looks as if everyone is here now," I say, as I see my parents hop out of Amanda and Bruce's SUV. Other church members follow in their footsteps until they reach Mrs. Diaz. We are told once again to cover certain sections and to walk in a slow line scouring the ground.

Several things turn up during the search. My group finds a watch, which is taken in for evidence, although Natalie assures me it isn't hers. It's discovered someone has been dumping trash out in the woods, which is illegal and will certainly be investigated. Other things are found, including one random adult man's shoe.

Some bones are unearthed when one of the searchers sees something poking out of a bed of leaves but two points are made to discount their relevance. A few avid hunters guarantee they are animal bones but they are still taken in for analysis and point two, being that Natalie has only been missing for a little over forty-eight hours; her body wouldn't decompose that quickly. Both are good points.

Most of us head to the diner for sandwiches. I check in with Piper who has heard the sheriff has questioned several girls from school. The cops wanted to speak to Ben but he wasn't home and Kooky made sure they didn't step foot on his property without a warrant. I filled Piper in on the news Camden told me about the missing girl from Nampa but she had already heard the report.

I can't believe how fast time has gone today. It's already getting dark. I leave the diner and start heading home. A nice hot shower is calling my name. My mind is preoccupied, though, with trying to figure out how Natalie was killed. Why did no one find any real evidence today during our search?

"What if your body was moved?"

Seeing as I started this conversation with no prelude to my thoughts, Natalie gives the proper response:

"Huh?"

"Like, what if you were attacked on your way home near where we found your earring but you were taken somewhere else? That could explain why no one found anything today."

"Oh. That's a good point. I never thought about it that way."

"Do you remember being taken or tortured or anything else?"

"No. I remember walking home and then it was blackness."

I can feel her straining, as she seems to be trying to remember something.

"Do you think the missing girl from Nampa is still alive? What did Piper say her name was?" I ask Natalie.

135

"Olivia Lane."

"Yeah, that was it. Can you like, call upon other spirits?"

"I've not tried that one yet."

"OK. Well, try it."

In a loud voice Natalie calls out, "Olivia Lane. If you're out there, please let us know. We'd like to ask you a few questions about how you died."

For once, Natalie doesn't have even a hint of sarcasm in her voice. Guess she does want some answers.

Silence.

"Maybe your voice only stays in my head. Maybe other spirits can't even hear you. Let me try."

I say the exact same words Natalie said, and still no response.

"Maybe Olivia isn't dead?"

"Hmm. Yeah," I agree.

As I'm driving, I realize I'm not driving in the direction of home. I missed my turn about ten minutes back.

"Crap, Natalie. I'm not even going the right way home."

"Do a u-ey. No one is around."

As I make a wide U-turn, I see a light in the distance and faint smoke in the air. Not too unusual to see that in the woods. People camp all the time but this isn't campground property; it's private property. It's the property I was at yesterday after I left Andrea's house and Natalie told me to go to the hot spring.

"What's that?" I ask rhetorically. "It looks like it's coming from the cave next to the hot spring."

"Yeah." I can imagine Natalie standing on her tippy-toes and squinting her eyes to get a better look.

"I think someone is at your hot spring."

I search around, not seeing any cars along the roadside. I look further into the woods and find a truck parked probably near the cave where I sheltered during the rainstorm.

"That's Kooky's truck," Natalie alerts me.

I try to come up with a perfectly good reason for him being in the woods. "He's probably hunting."

"Why would he go on private property?" Natalie asks and I can almost feel the lightbulb going off as she continues. "V, he was brought in for questioning this morning. What if he knows he's about to be caught and is about to kill that Olivia girl? You have to go help her," she pleads.

I can feel her anxiety overwhelming my body and affecting my mind. Her desperation is evident and I know I can't hold onto my own emotions for much longer.

I turn out my headlights and pull over. I put on the hoodie I keep in the backseat and jump out of the car. I start running into the woods. I have no plan, no weapons, no clear thoughts, just the drive. *Some girl may need me to interfere and save her life but what if I lose my own during that process? I wonder what will happen to Natalie's spirit if I die. Does she go to the next available person?*

"Slow down. You don't want Kooky to hear you."

I stop running and slowly make my way toward the fire inside the cave.

137

After her slight interruption, my body loses some of its ammo and my recent nightmare comes flooding into my mind. I am already scared. I don't need the thought of John Harper running after me in the woods to play over and over in my mind, especially when that could happen in the next few minutes. I see a decent-sized rock and pick it up. I don't quite have a plan for it but I'm certain it will at least let me injure the man.

My breath is ragged and the adrenaline that was dwindling is back in full bloom now that I have a weapon. My eyes are searching everywhere, looking for Kooky or his victim. I inch closer to the cave and whisper to Natalie, "Keep quiet so I can listen to our surroundings."

Chapter 9

Sucker Punch

Natalie agrees to keep quiet. My body is trembling with fear. Would he hurt me, too? I reject that thought immediately. Be brave, this is for Natalie, I chant to myself and possibly for Olivia. As I walk in, ready to attack, a glance at the silhouette of his face catches me off guard and I stand frozen. He turns his head slowly toward me, only enough to see me peripherally. There are tears running down his cheek. I don't understand what is going on. Why is he just sitting here? Where is Olivia?

Natalie's craving to comfort him is overwhelming but my sense of fear and confusion has my feet planted firmly. I swallowed hard and loud.

"I'm glad you're here." His voice is dry and raspy.

I wait quietly, not knowing what he means by that.

He turns his face back toward the small fire. I see something glisten in his hand. It looks to be an earring, the very match to the earring in my pocket, the earring of my newly dead friend, Natalie Knight. With fear taking over, I turn and start running. I hear him get up to run after me.

"Wait," he yells and grabs the hood of my hoodie. I twist around, throwing my fists any which way I can, screaming in his face to let me go. I hit him in the head with the rock. It doesn't faze him. I release the rock and begin to tear at his face with my nails, never making contact because he grabs my wrists and pulls me with him as we fall to the ground. He's sobbing.

"I didn't mean to. I didn't mean to, I'm sorry. I'm sorry." He continues sobbing. Tears are streaming down his face.

Still holding my wrists tightly, he begs, "Please. Let me tell you what happened. Please."

I sit awkwardly but say severely, "Let go of me."

"OK." He looks into my eyes pleading. "But, please, let me explain. Please."

I nod my head and he releases my wrists. They tingle as the blood rushes through them. I jump up and back away to allow space. I have no other choice; we need to know the truth. I quiver, "Go ahead, Ben."

He stays on his knees as if asking for forgiveness.

Squeezing his eyes shut, he confesses. "I didn't see her. I didn't see her, I swear," he says. He continues to cry but gains a little control and begins his story.

"Thursday night I was driving home from Slim's. We had been swimming all day and my brain was a little fried. Natalie was the only thing I talked about that day. Slim said I was whining about her but whatever." He sniffs. "I couldn't get her off my mind. I liked her so much and her mom was so pissed at us when she caught us in Nat's bed. We didn't even sleep together." He reaches his arm up to grab my arm in a pleading attempt for understanding but thinks better of it and grabs air, making a fist instead. "I mean, we were sleeping but we hadn't, you know, had sex or anything," he clarifies. He is talking so fast it's hard to focus. "Her mom screamed at me to get out and said she was gonna call the cops on me. You know, 'cause I'm eighteen.

She said it was statutory rape. She wouldn't even listen to Natalie. Natalie kept screaming, 'Nothing happened' but she wouldn't listen to us. She was so angry and kept screaming at me to get out.

"Anyway, I was driving home from Slim's and thinking about what I could say to Nat's mom to make all this misunderstanding go away. The sun was setting and it blinded me when I came around the corner, so I threw the visor down. I guess I swerved the truck a little and all of a sudden I hit something." He started breaking down again.

It's a strange thing to watch someone cry and have the emotions of fear, sadness, disgust and the urge to hug them all coursing through me but I remain frozen and just listen. He continues through the tears but not speaking as fast or as urgently as before.

"I figured I hit a deer. I got out and I saw the blood." He pauses, a grave look on his face. "Then I saw her. I knew. I ran over to her anyway and asked if she was OK. Over and over I asked her. Thinking miraculously she would wake up but she didn't. She lay there, dead. I put my head on her chest, wishing for a heartbeat. There was none. I carried her to the bed of my truck." He pauses for a moment and I can see the anguish in his face. I sit down finally and hope he will continue. I'm not feeling as scared anymore. Maybe the adrenaline is calming down and fatigue is setting in.

"I headed toward the hospital, even though I knew it was too late but I needed to do something, right? Tell someone, right? I had so many thoughts running through my head and there it was. I knew Natalie's mom would say I did it on purpose, that it was a fit of rage, that I was angry at Kandi because she tried to keep us apart, or something. She already threatened to call the cops on me.

"Now that Natalie was dead, people would say I'm just like my father, the rumors of my father, anyway. So I went into the woods and laid her body on the ground. I spoke to her for a bit, telling her how beautiful she was and that I was so sorry. I told her this was the only way. No one would believe me. So I kissed her cheek and took her earring."

He looks over at me. "I didn't know the other one was missing until I saw you picking it up." He looks into the fire and repeats himself, "I kissed her cheek and took her earring, and I burned her body." His face wears a look of disgust and he clenches his jaw. "I grabbed a handful of her ashes and threw them into the lake. I officially became the rumors of my father. He didn't kill my mom, you know."

I don't nod. I just stare at him.

As he continues looking into the fire I speak softly but with all the conviction I have within me. "Ben?"

He looks at me expectantly. "You have to turn yourself in. I know initially it was an accident. Everyone knows she's missing. You need to turn yourself in." I wait for his reaction, not knowing what to expect. He nods his head in agreement but it's not too convincing. It looks as if he is trying to figure something out.

"How did you know? I didn't even know you knew her. How did you know she was missing before anybody else knew?" he asks again.

This is a situation that can easily lead to getting myself in trouble. I have her earring; the same as he has her other earring. I can't tell him the truth. If I did, he could tell the world the crazy diner waitress murdered his girlfriend and thinks she has her spirit within her. I have to be careful with what I say to him. I can't let him know I've known for three nights Natalie has been dead; not missing, but dead. I can't tell him I sneaked onto his property and broke into his dad's shed because I thought his dad was the murderer. I can't tell him I saw Natalie's cell phone in that shed, either. I guess Ben put it in there.

I don't have to say anything to Ben but for some reason I choose to.

"I work at the diner and her mom, Kandi, came in sad and talking about the fight between her and Natalie. Kandi told me Natalie was staying at her friend, Andrea's house, and Kandi was supposed to give them a ride to the bonfire. Natalie wasn't answering her calls, so I said I would go over there to see if I could drive them to the bonfire. Turns out Natalie wasn't there. When I was at the bonfire last night I saw she wasn't with you. I had heard you guys had been hanging out recently."

Ben confides, "I was there to see if you knew about what happened because I saw you picking up her earring."

I had no idea he saw me. I try to think quickly to give a response. I also try to remember I don't owe him any explanations. I'm not the guilty one here.

"I was too early to pick them up for the bonfire, so I took a little walk. I saw the earring and picked it up but I didn't know it was Natalie's until you just told me," I add, in another lie to make the story complete. "When I saw the fire here, I thought maybe it was Natalie. So I came to see if I could convince her to go home."

"With a rock in your hand?"

"In case it wasn't Natalie."

I don't know how good of a lie I have told. Who knows if he is even listening to me closely? I don't think I've said anything suspicious. I keep going over what I have said in my mind so that I can remember it, in case I need to retell my side of the story.

We sit in silence for quite a while. Every few minutes his mood changes. Sometimes I can see relief on his face. Other times I could see the weight of his actions is sinking in. He runs his hands through his hair and looks down for minutes at a time, the grief on his face and the agony. He looks tired and sweaty, vulnerable even.

The changes between the man who was chasing me to the young man seeking redemption to the boy who now looks destroyed; these transformations are making my head spin. I can't seem to piece together all the emotions going through me. I don't know which are mine and which are Natalie's.

"Hey, V?" a very meek and sad voice calls to me.

I look up so she knows I am acknowledging her. So she asks, "Can you ask him why he took my earring?"

I nod.

"Ben?" My voice is hoarse from screaming.

"Yeah?" he says, wiping his face. He takes a deep breath and looks up at me.

"Why did you take her earring?"

He looks away rather quickly. Is he grinning? I can't tell.

"Natalie was wearing them the first time we met." He looks back at me with a sincere smile and, *oh, yes, he must have been grinning because his face is a little flushed.*

"At a basketball game," they say at the same time.

"The earring fell out of her ear when she was walking near me and I picked it up for her. When I handed it to her…I don't know…she was beautiful. Her smile was amazing. From then on I was hooked. I wanted to know everything about her. We would talk on the phone for hours. I wanted to be around her all the time. She was so…funny. So funny," he adds again, with a small laugh.

I can't take my eyes off him. *He seems so genuine, so sincere, so…in love.* My head is still spinning. *I didn't expect any of this. Ben and not*

John, being scared to death, his painful confession, and now his loving confession.

After a long moment of silence he stands up and kicks dirt onto the fire.

"I guess I better get to the sheriff's."

He walks past me and gets into his father's truck and drives off.

I quickly acknowledge the missing Olivia has nothing to do with Natalie's death. I hope she's OK.

"Are you OK?" I ask Natalie quietly.

"I can't believe it was Ben. Obviously, I wish things would have worked out differently. I wish I were still alive. I wish my mom would have trusted me and left it alone. I wish I could..." She pauses for a moment and says, "You know, it sucks all around."

"Yeah, I'm sorry, Natalie." I don't know what else to say.

"I'm glad it wasn't malicious."

"It was a hit-and-run, Natalie. And by run, I mean he ran to burn your body."

She's silent for a minute. *My emotions are running amuck. I can't tell if she's hurt, angry, or confused. Factor in my own emotions of having just listened to a confession and I have a headache of feelings. Spending so much time together, I am starting to feel her emotions so much more intensely. If we are together long enough, will our souls melt and become one fluid being?*

"V," she speaks gently. I must have hurt her feelings. "I mean that he didn't seek me out to murder me. I know what he did was wrong." She lightens up a little. "Hello. I'm the dead one here.

You saw him, V. He was scared and it was already too late for me. He needed to save himself at that point, ya know. I understand. I do. I guess there's something to be said about the element of surprise."

"We've all had our share of that lately." I smile as I tell her this, recalling my own reactions the past few days.

"Yeah. No one knows what they would do in that situation. I'm sure he never thought he would do something like that."

I mull over that comment for a moment and think how true it is. *We could all say what we would do or could do if that ever happened to us; but really? Most people probably imagine themselves as heroes in certain scenarios and maybe even give themselves a lot of credit about how rational they would be if they're ever in that situation but you have no real idea until you are in it. Would I have ever thought I would be possessed? No. Because of that possession, would I have ever thought I would help solve a murder? No. Because of that murder, would I have ever thought I would confront the murderer? Absolutely not. I myself was thrown into a situation and in the beginning didn't handle it too well. Toward the end I became, well, I guess insane about following a murderer. Still not rational. Technically, now that I'm thinking about it, he's not a murderer. He accidentally hit her with his truck. Pretty much everything after that was wrong but it started as an accident.*

"Well, what's done is done," she says bluntly.

"Why didn't I ever ask you why you got into a fight with your mom? Why didn't you tell me?"

"I didn't know it would be so important. It probably would have led us straight to Kooky, which is where we ended up anyway," Natalie reasons

"Guess that's true," Victoria replies.

I feel a pulling sensation from deep inside me.

Chapter 10

New Beginnings

"It's time for me to go," she whispers quietly. I feel the pulling again. I look down at my hands. *It feels as if someone or something has taken her hand and is trying to guide her out of me. Out of this world. I start to panic. What is going to happen? I'm scared. Am I going to die? Maybe when Natalie's gone, my spirit will go, too.* I banish this thought from my mind, so I can remain calm.

I've grown so attached to her, hearing her inside me, her laugh, and her sense of humor. My heart starts racing. I feel I'm about to lose my little sister.

"Are you scared?" I ask, choking up. My lip starts to quiver, and tears roll down my face.

149

"No," she says confidently. "I feel peace."

My body instantly relaxes, and there's a surge of calm. My emotions are not my own.

"Thank you for risking your life for me, for sharing your life with me. I'm going to miss you so much. We're not even 'blood' sisters; we're like, 'soul' sisters," she giggles.

I'm going to miss that giggle.

"Oh, Natalie, I wouldn't change knowing you like this. I love you so much." My body has no other feeling than calm. I can't seem to fight or override the feeling. I wrap my arms around my torso, hugging tightly. I don't want to let her go. "Maybe you can stay. You can repel again."

"Don't be silly, V. We would kill each other. Well, you know what I mean."

Another tug.

Natalie continues, "I love you, too. Take care of yourself. Think of me when you go swimming."

"I will. And when I see a rainbow." I smile.

"I have to go *Irish* 'for cryin' out loud,'" she says, taking my line.

"*Liam Neeson*," I whisper.

I feel another tug at my feet, my legs, my stomach and shoulders, my hands, my arms and my head. There's a burning sensation on my wrist. I look down but there's nothing there. Only extreme pain. I grab my wrist and squeeze it. Tears stream down my face for more than one reason now. I scream as the pain heats up even more. *I've never been burned with a red-hot poker but I imagine this is what it's like.* I continue squeezing my wrist and slam into a tree. I

150

clench my eyes shut, wishing it would stop. My chest rises toward the sky and my head falls back. I almost feel as if I am being lifted off the ground a little. Then nothing.

Everything seems to stop all at once.

No voice.

No giggle.

No burning.

No pulling.

Empty.

"Natalie?"

My friend, my sister is gone. I fall to the ground, my own emotions returning in full force. I cry uncontrollably. My body shakes violently. *Such a beautiful young life that should never have been taken. The hole in my heart will never be filled. I will never be that close to anyone again.* I release my wrist and punch the ground with my fist in anger and sorrow. I repeat her name over and over, hoping she will answer back. Finally, my body stops shaking and I lie there sobbing.

After a long period of time, I open my eyes. I must have fallen asleep because the sun is breaking over the horizon. I get up slowly and brush myself off. I feel all the aches and pains from sleeping on the ground and from being so tense during my encounter with Ben. I slowly walk back toward my car. When I reach to grab the handle, I see rays of color on my wrist. I blink several, times trying to focus on it. I certainly recall the searing pain from under my skin. In its place is a bunch of squiggly lines, colors of the rainbow. Why in the world would I have such a mark? I gently rub it, thinking maybe it will come off. It doesn't even smudge. I can only speculate maybe it's a warrior wound. *I was chosen as Natalie's host. I accepted that challenge and carried it through to the end, helping her with her unfinished business.* My mind gets distracted by that thought. I hope Ben actually went to the authorities last night instead of making a run for it. I stare at the lines, tracing them with my finger. *This mark is my friend, Natalie, a beautiful reminder that she was here. A rainbow to remember her.* I wipe a single tear from my cheek and get in my car.

Back at home, I quietly walk up to my room, so as not to wake my parents and I pass out on my bed.

Chapter 11

Ben's Big Mouth

No one knows about my, for lack of a better word, possession, but Ben mentions my name during his confession to the sheriff. Residents and the sheriff think I'm some kind of Nancy Drew, sounds as if someone spoke to Natalie. So naturally they want to speak with me. I tell the sheriff Kandi told me things at the diner; about her fight with Natalie, Natalie was staying at Andrea's house. I couldn't get it out of my mind because Kandi was so upset. I went to Andrea's house to see if I could drive them to the bonfire and convince Natalie to go home but it was obvious Natalie wasn't there. I had no idea Ben saw me pick up the earring. I never thought of calling the police over an earring and I thought Natalie was with Ben, anyway.

The sheriff doesn't ask me if I still have the earring, which is a relief. I have bigger plans for that earring than letting it sit in the sheriff's office.

I also tell them she wasn't at the bonfire that night and she wasn't with her boyfriend. Of course, I leave out the part about me going to Ben's house because Natalie and I thought his dad had killed her. I went to help with the search at Kent Woods and then to the diner to get a sandwich. As I drove home, I saw John Harper's truck on the side of the road. No one was in it. I noticed what seemed to be a glowing firelight in the cave near the hot spring, so I put on my brave pants and walked over to the cave.

I honestly did not have a clue as to what I was going to do. I was just suspicious and wanted to see if Natalie was with John. I knew John had been taken in for questioning and I thought maybe he was up to no good out there. Ben had seen me at the scene of the accident. He knew I had brought Andrea to the bonfire, so he assumed I realized she was missing and was piecing everything together. That's one reason he confessed to me. The other reason was he was ready to be free of what had happened and knew Natalie deserved better. It was only a matter of time.

Over the past few days, there have been many arguments and controversy regarding Ben. Some people want to burn him at the stake. He's a murderer, simple as that but I know differently. I saw with my own eyes the agony and the sorrow Ben feels. I truly know it was an accident and he was simply a frightened young man. He made a horrible decision but it was out of fear and desperation.

I believe he cares tremendously for Natalie. The element of surprise and being in a state of panic can make anyone's reaction confusing and damning. Ben's shock over the accident and the thoughts running through his head overwhelmed him and led him into making a not so brilliant decision. Many people want to see him go to prison, either because of his decision to burn the dead body or because of a belief his actions were intentional.

For some reason, certain people just won't allow it was an accident that kept getting worse. It's a tough situation for me. On one hand, I don't want people to believe lies about him and, on the other hand, I don't want people to think I condone his behavior; his decision to burn the body and not tell anyone for days.

I wonder how Kandi sees it.

So, besides my interview with the sheriff, I'm keeping my mouth shut. I will never talk about it again.

I am allowed a little peace. Reporters have been knocking at our door nonstop since my interview. They want to interview me and hear the chilling details of how I escaped the grasp of the Burton Killer. Ridiculous.

Piper won't stop calling and texting me. I need some space and some time to mourn and Piper seems to understand this but only for so long then she is at my house, pounding on the door. Mom lets her in but because I won't speak much, she stays downstairs with my parents. I can't tell them the truth that I'm mourning the loss of Natalie, so I asked them to please let me deal with the aftermath of my encounter with Ben privately. I've cried for several days and I hope by releasing all that emotion I've drained myself so I'm able to attend the church service. I can't be seen bawling in church, having not known her publicly.

Mom and Piper are coming to the service to support me and act as shields to deflect reporters.

I put on my black dress pants with a matching black lightweight jacket and a dark purple blouse. Purple was Natalie's favorite color. I have to stop for a moment to catch my breath, not that I've exerted myself, but any memory sneaking its way into my thoughts still stings. I swallow hard and sit on the chair in the corner of the room. I slowly inhale through my nose and exhale out of my mouth. I do this several times, until I feel I've calmed down a little. I don't have a true comparison but I associate my loss of Natalie with that of losing a friend or sister or a child. I didn't know it would affect me so much.

I buckle on a pair of black dressy sandals and head to the bathroom. I brush my hair and leave it down and put on my makeup. Concealer. Not sure if this is part of the mourning process but I keep hearing Natalie's voice in my head, inserting sarcastic remarks where I think she would have said them. At least it makes me smile.

Mom is waiting in the living room for me when I arrive downstairs. She is wearing a beautiful classy black dress that goes to her knees, black dressy sandals, and a silvery gray wrap.

"Piper is in the car in the garage so we aren't photographed."

"Are you OK?" she asks softly.

I nod.

"Yeah. It's a sad situation all around. I feel for Kandi and what she must be going through."

She nods while her eyes fill with tears, thinking no doubt she too could be in Kandi's position right now. My parents were rightfully hysterical when they found out I was the person who found Ben.

We arrive at the church. The whole town is here. There are beautiful flower arrangements everywhere. At the front of the pulpit are big pictures of Natalie: a profile of her laughing while at the lake, another showing her as a kid beside her brother with ice cream all over their faces and one big one right in the center with a beautiful mum arrangement underneath. This has her smiling shyly at the camera with her long straight red hair tucked behind her ears, showing off her earrings, the earrings her dad gave her for Christmas. They are stunning diamonds and they shimmer on her. I can feel many eyes focused on me and that is probably the reason Piper's grip on my arm has gotten tighter. Protective mode. I walk with my head bowed, Mom and Piper on either side of me.

We are ushered to a pew in the back of the church as we requested. Through rows of people, I can see Kandi, a young man to her left, who is Natalie's brother, I assume, and an older man to her right, probably Natalie's father. Someone whispers to Kandi and she, in turn, murmurs to both men beside her then all three turn around to look at me.

Kandi looks frail with pale skin and tears running down her face. Her hair is just as beautiful as the photo shows Natalie's to have been: long and straight strawberry blonde. The older man, evidently

Natalie's father, is seemingly a tall man with a full head of salt-and-pepper hair. Natalie favors her dad facially but has the build and red hair of her mother. Her father, of course, looks beside himself with grief. The young man, who I assume is Natalie's brother, seems tall and has thick dark brown hair. My breath catches as I realize how much he looks like Natalie. It's a resemblance in the eyes and the nose, just like the father. Her brother looks broken. Kandi smiles at me kindly: it's an unspoken 'Thank You'. I give her a small smile in return and nod then they turn around.

A small group gathers at the front of the pulpit. They sing "Amazing Grace". There is a mother/daughter duo singing alto, an older man singing tenor and a young woman singing soprano. The *a capella* mix tugs at the heartstrings. They finish the hymn and I'm not sure there is a dry eye in the church. The minister walks up to the pulpit and thanks the choral group.

My heart is beating out of my chest and it's hard to breathe. I have to keep my head down so I don't see her picture. It's too painful. Suddenly my mind is filled with conversations Natalie and I had. Her voice is still in the forefront of my subconscious.

"You can't shake me out of your head, silly."

"Can I make you involuntarily slap yourself?"

"Is it creepy if I were to say you're growing in me, I mean on me?"

"Ew. You make me sound like a fungus."

"Stop, V. Stop. Not here." I chant these words in my head over and over so I can pull it together.

There are several prayers, scripture readings and even the sharing of memories by people who approach the pulpit to tell a funny or sweet story involving Natalie.

After the final prayer, Mom, Piper and I stand and immediately leave the auditorium. I'm feeling much more relieved now the service is over. I think the anticipation of going put a great deal of anxiety on me.

A short time later, my boss, Mike, and I gather some of the food trays at the diner and load them in the car to take to the funeral reception at Kandi's house. A relative has ordered penne, salad, bread and sodas. Piper insisted that she help Mike with the reception but I told her I want to go. I have something I want to give to Natalie's parents.

"You doing OK, V?" Mike asks, as he drives away from the diner.

"Yeah, I'm all right. I don't care much for all the attention but it'll go away soon."

We drive the rest of the way in silence. I look out the window without seeing anything. I try to keep my nerves in check, so I can do this job and talk to Natalie's parents without any drama. I assume this will be an uneventful visit in that they acknowledged me at the church but you never know. I'm not sure how they feel about my opinion regarding Ben. Everyone knows I defended Ben. Emotions run high when there's a death.

We arrive at a beautiful home that fits right into the country setting. It's white and has a big porch out in front with one of those swings that hang from the ceiling. I'm always afraid I'm going to break one of those.

Cars are lined up all over the block but a spot is saved for us in the driveway. I take a deep breath and get out.

As I lift one of the trays, someone calls out,

"Can I help you with that?" and Natalie's brother comes over, along with a man standing next to him.

"Uh, sure," I reply and he takes the tray from me and hands it to the man next to him. He directs him to put it in the kitchen. I turn and pull out another tray and hand this one to him too, before grabbing one for myself and following him and Mike into the kitchen.

"Thank you for helping," I say to him.

"Of course." He turns his head to the side so I can hear him from behind. He has a deep voice. It reminds me of Matt Damon.

"Are you Natalie's brother?" I lean my head forward so he can hear me better.

"Yeah."

I thought so. We set the trays on the counter, and he turns to me.

"I'm Damien," he says. "Is there anything else I can help you with?"

"No. No, it's our job, sir," Mike interjects kindly. "V, go grab the bags of ice while I set this up."

I nod to him. I head out the door and pull two bags of ice from the back seat and when I turn around, I almost scream. Damien has followed me.

"Oh, sorry. I didn't mean to scare you. Let me take those. You're the famous Victoria?" he asks gently.

"Everyone calls me V," I say and smile at him, seeing as we can't shake hands because his are full.

We walk back to the kitchen, side by side this time.

160

"Thank you for what you did. You didn't actually know Natalie, did you?" He seems a little confused, probably trying to understand my involvement.

"No. After seeing Kandi so upset, I thought I'd try to help out a little, maybe talk Natalie into going home. Once I pieced everything together, I thought either Kooky was involved or she ran away. I never expected to come face-to-face with Ben and have him confess to me." I shiver at the memory of Ben running after me in the woods. Damien looks down at me with anger in his eyes. Oh, my. What did I say? Was it because I said Ben's name? Stupid. I should be more considerate. I spoke his name too lightly.

As we enter the kitchen, he says quietly through gritted teeth, "And you don't think he did it on purpose?"

OK, so he knows about my report. He opens the ice and dumps it into buckets with more force than necessary, making me flinch. A few people shoot a glance our way but continue with their conversations. I stand there nervous but I know what I saw in Ben's eyes; his confession and anguish and how he felt about Natalie.

"I'm sorry," I say, trying to diffuse his anger a little. I say it for the offense caused by my belief in Ben, for the loss of his sister, for the pain he feels and the inconsiderateness I showed in my earlier mentioning of his name.

"It's not your fault," he scoffs.

He leans on the table with both hands grabbing the edge and his head down.

"I'm just so angry, we didn't even get to say goodbye to her," he spits through his teeth. I look around nervously. I have no idea what to do. I don't know if he's going to throw the bucket of ice or fall to his knees and start crying. As I'm looking around, the man who helped him carry the food trays seems to understand my silent alarm. He looks at Damien and makes his way over to us.

"Hey, cuz," he says gently. "Let's go for a walk, man." He puts a hand on Damien's upper back and Damien looks up at him. He's shaking with anger. Damien nods to his cousin and they head out the door without a second glance in my direction.

Relieved to be out of that situation, I get back to work, grabbing the empty bags of ice and helping Mike to finish setting-up. When we are done, we give our condolences to Jim, Natalie's father and to Kandi, who hugs me for a long time.

"You are a brave young woman," she cries into my ear.

Again, I'm at a loss for words so I remain silent. I'd like to say, *No I'm not brave. I'm stupid, actually. Who goes after a grown man in the woods, alone with no weapons? What idiot doesn't call the cops?*

She releases me from our embrace but holds me at arm's length at my shoulders. Jim's hand is at the small of her back, a very loving gesture. "Thank you, Victoria, for trying to save Natalie. We didn't know she was already taken from us. Whether it was an accident or not, I don't think he would have confessed if it weren't for you. I'm glad you didn't get hurt as well." Her lip quivers and I can see how hard she is trying to stay composed.

I believe Ben would have confessed without him seeing me grab the earring, without him seeing me with Andrea and without me accidentally tracking him down in the cave. I hold my tongue; I learned my lesson for the day.

She pulls me in for a hug once more and says, "You are welcome here anytime. You are like family now. Please stop by sometime, Victoria." She releases me completely and I nod at her through teary eyes.

"Bye, Ms. Knight, Mr. Knight." I nod in both their directions and shake Mr. Knight's hand. He looks in his palm after I release my hand. He stares at me with wet but elated eyes.

"She would want you to have it."

He holds out the earring he gave Natalie for Christmas the year before.

"Thank you."

He smiles and I head out the door after Mike.

Chapter 12

Giving Thanks

I visit my old co-workers at the diner. I can't believe it's already been three months since I was here. Suzy is still working hard at the register, Diane is still as moody as ever and Mike has hired two new waiters. One, a junior this year and another a senior—both good-looking guys who will no doubt bring in all the ladies, young and old.

The town seems back to normal. Main Street is now decorated with festive wreaths and lights instead of ribbons and balloons, hoping for the safe return of Natalie. In a few days, the town will be adorned with Christmassy decorations and the stores will all compete for the best window display.

I make my way to the grocery store because my mom needs more food for Thanksgiving.

My brother is bringing his fiancé. They have been dating for three years. They were separated several times because the Navy stationed them in different places. They are both being stationed in the same place this time and they've decided they want to get married before they leave. They aren't looking for a huge wedding or anything fancy. They just want to get hitched as, Violet, so eloquently put it. She has such a soft name, for such a powerful person. Not only is she fierce and completely made of muscle, she competes in something equivalent to the cross fit games on base. She won second place this last tournament. She is super determined to be first place next time around. Leave it to my brother to find an awesome partner in life and also have her first name begin with a V. My parents love her to death.

Valentina is having her boyfriend over as well. I can smell an engagement coming soon there, too. She's all hot and bothered by him. Whatever.

I wish I had someone to bring but I won't dwell on that, I'm only nineteen.

I walk into the grocery store and head over to the baking aisle. I check the text message for the items she needs:

Brown Sugar

Eggs

Butter

As I'm squatting down grabbing the brown sugar, I see out of the corner of my eye, a pair of jeans and sneakers stop next to me.

"Hey?" The wearer asks.

I look up expecting an old high school buddy and I am shocked, as I register who it is.

I can only choke out one word, "Damien."

I stand up.

My heart aches, as I stare at Natalie's brother. His hands are in his pockets and he's smiling at me. He looks relieved but I have no idea why. He looks, well, gorgeous. A lot better than the broken man I saw at his sister's funeral.

"How are you?" I whisper.

"I'm good." He looks down and leans back on his heels. We are staring at each other like a couple of idiots.

"Are you home for Thanksgiving?" I ask.

"Yeah. You?"

"Yep. We drove in last night."

"We?" He furrows his brow. He seems nervous, so I answer quickly.

"My roommate, Piper. Who happens to also be my best friend since we were born."

"Oh. Cool," he sighs heavily. "Was she the one with you at the funeral?"

"Yeah, she was. My mom was with me, too."

He looks up to think, probably trying to remember their faces. "I was in her math class years ago."

"Oh, small world." I try to keep the conversation going but redirect it. "What college are you going to?"

"Idaho State. I'm going to start the PT program next year."

"Oh, wow. A physical therapist. That's cool."

"Yeah, I've been in school forever it seems. Where do you go to college?"

As college school rivals, I hesitate. I give him a sheepish grin and reply, "Boise State." I scrunch my face, waiting for his reaction.

"Oh. I can't hear that," he laughs. "What's your major?"

"That's kind of up in the air right now. There was a gypsy at the bonfire and she told me my Grand Pappy, who died many years ago, told her to tell me to change my major. I was going to go for teaching but now I might be interested in doing private investigating, to help find missing children. I don't know yet."

Bless his heart that was a lot to take in. He kindly replies, "That seems to be your niche. You will be great at doing that kind of work."

A woman and her little daughter, excuse themselves between us to grab a bag of sugar. I walk around them apologizing and stand closer to Damien. I only have to lift my head a little to meet his eyes. The little girl squeals in excitement over sprinkles, which reminds me to ask Damien a question.

"Do you have family coming to your mom's house?"

"Yeah, a few cousins, aunts and uncles. Actually, my dad is coming in from the city."

"Oh," I say, in surprise.

"My parents have gotten closer since Natalie past."

I wince in pain hearing her name. I miss her.

"Oh, that's wonderful." I put on a smile.

He leans over and whispers, "I think my parents are dating." A huge grin crosses his face.

Surprised by his proximity, my mood instantly changes.

"I'm so glad to hear that," I suppress a giggle. He smells divine. Not too strong but a nice cologne. "Natalie would have been thrilled," I add softly.

"Yeah, she would have."

We continue smiling and staring at each other. I didn't notice before how beautiful his smile was; his teeth are perfe...

My phone vibrates in my hand and I jump, startled. I hold my phone to my heart in reaction. "Oh geez," I yell. "Sorry," I apologize to him for jumping and yelling.

"Your boyfriend probably wants you to hurry up?" He says, as more of a question than a comment.

"Oh, no. I don't have a boyfriend. It's my mom adding things to my shopping list. Vanilla Extract." I walk over, grab it and put it in my basket.

"Could I carry your basket for you?"

"Oh, no. I'm fine."

"I don't mind, Victoria." He extends his hand, and I nod, accepting his offer. I never knew my name was so beautiful. Why are butterflies swarming in my stomach?

"Thank you, Damien."

"My pleasure," he smiles sweetly. "What's next on your list?"

"Eggs," I say, without looking away from his gaze. He turns fractionally and ushers me next to him, so we can walk side-by-side.

"I wanted to apologize for my behavior at the reception. I was on edge and angry. I've gone to counseling, which has helped a lot. I don't blame Ben, anymore, which is a big step. Maybe, even the biggest step to overcome."

I look up at him in shock.

"I don't like him but I don't blame him either," he qualifies. "If I saw him, I'd probably still punch him. It was an accident. Anyway," he clears his throat, "I wanted to apologize for making you feel..." he hesitates..."however, I made you feel."

It's a touching moment, to see someone who apparently is uncomfortable apologizing for his actions, actually open up and do it.

"Accepted." Maybe that was the awkwardness hovering around us earlier. Our space seems less stressed now. "So, what's on your list, Mr. Knight?"

"Potatoes, celery and wine but I'm not sure we will be doing much eating. It's our first Thanksgiving without her. It's going to be..." he pauses..."sad."

I stop in front of the eggs and look up at him. "Oh, Natalie wouldn't want that," I say softly.

"I know," he looks down at me gently. "But it will be."

I grab the eggs, and ask, "Is your mom up to cooking?"

"Kandi? Cook?" he scoffs, lightening the mood. "No, my dad and I are the ones who cook."

I guess that's the reason Kandi always came to the diner. I turn and stare at him, in amazement. "Are you any good?" I ask, before I can stop myself.

"Of, course," he says confidently, not fazed by my audacity. When he takes the eggs from me, our fingers touch. Neither of us release the eggs, we stand there and stare at each other. Something strange happens. It feels as a jolt of lightning running through my veins. In this moment, I feel as if I can see clearly. Life makes sense, the stars are aligned and I feel happy. All of those books I've read about men dazzling women, fireworks and electric currents. This is mine. This is my story right here.

Oh, crap, am I sweating? I'm sweating and we're in the refrigerator section.

Irish

'For cryin' out loud.'

'*Liam Neeson.*'

I can't seem to say one, without the other, anymore. Not even in my subconscious.

Thoughts of Natalie overwhelm me and a huge smile crosses my face at the memory. He smiles in return but I quickly wipe the smile from my face in embarrassment. Oh, man. He thinks I was grinning because we touched.

He puts the eggs in the basket; "I'd love to cook for you sometime," his look is serious now yet hopeful.

"I would like that," I try to disguise my excitement and the urge to ask when? I look down to control my anxiety.

"What's next?" he whispers near my ear.

Marriage? I forget what we were even talking about. I look at him confused.

"On your list," he laughs.

Oh. Hello V. Look alive. "Butter."

We stroll through the aisles, not paying attention to anyone around us. We talk about professors and exams. We discover we have in common a love of skiing and speedboats. I ignore the constant buzzing of my pocket. Ultimately, we finish both of our lists.

Damien pays for all of them and walks me to my car.

"When do you want to cook for me?" Apparently, I can't refrain.

"How about Saturday? Unless you have plans."

"Oh, no plans. That would be perfect." Piper will totally understand my cancelling our movie date.

"My mom will be delighted to see you. She talks about you all the time."

"Does she? That's sweet. I can't wait to see her, too." I stare into his eyes, secretly telling him I can't wait to see him Saturday.

Kandi and I have talked several times on the phone during the semester. She reminds me a lot of Natalie so I try to talk to her often.

We exchange phone numbers and say "bye."

I get in my car, and immediately text Piper.

Pipe. I have a date Saturday night...Let's do brunch Sunday...

No less than 20 seconds go by and my phone is ringing. I knew she'd call.

Epilogue

"I can't believe the school year is over," I say, thrilled.

"I know. Our first year over and done." Piper gives a fake pout.

I am compiling a list of things we need for our summer vacation. Valentina's new fiancé, Ted, insisted on paying for everyone's tickets. His dad has a lot of money, it seems.

"I can't wait until the fall," I say, while doodling on the summer vacation list.

"Oh, yes, that's right. Damien got his transfer to Boise State and he got into the Physical Therapy program?"

"Yeah. He packed up all his stuff, and finished his last semester at Idaho State."

"Booo…" Piper interjects. We just can't like a rival school.

"It was all really fast and yet it doesn't feel rushed at all, if that makes sense."

"Of course, it makes sense."

"I can't wait. You and I get to live off-campus in our own apartment and Damien will be in the same town at the same school. It's going to be perfect."

"Yes, it will be. Now stop fast forwarding my summer." Piper complains and turns up the radio.

I find time alone to make a stop at Natalie's gravesite.

"Hey, Natalie. I can't believe it's been nine months since we were sharing a body together," I giggle. "I wanted to say I miss you so much and I love you." I rub my wrist where my colorful squiggly rainbow is. "School is out and I can't wait to go on vacation. We're all going to Ireland. It's going to be amazing. I'm stopping by your house this evening to see your mom. She wants to show off her wedding pictures. I'm so glad your parents got back together. I think it will work out for them this time. Your brother will be coming into town tomorrow. I hope you're happy for your brother and me. We're happy." I sniff as tears begin to fall.

"I like him so much, Natalie. Well, love him. I'm so glad you came into my life and, if you sent him to me, thank you. Look at me; I'm a running mascara mess.

Irish

'For cryin' out loud.'

'*Liam Neeson.*'"

About the Author

Meredith Baldwin is a wife, mother, writer, conjurer of way too many stories in her head, and is the author of Swallowed Ashes Victoria's Journey. This book started many years ago in middle school. It was put in a box and moved to several different places throughout Meredith's life. It was rediscovered in 2009. Meredith was busy having more children at the time, so it was put back into a box. In 2012 some real writing started to happen. This is the first book ever written by Meredith.

Made in the USA
Coppell, TX
30 November 2020